CATS OF ITALY

ALSO BY ANN REAVIS

Death at the Duomo

Italian Food Rules

Italian Life Rules

Murder at Mountain Vista

The Case of the Pilfered Pills

CATS OF ITALY

By
Ann Reavis

CATS OF ITALY

This is a work of fiction. Names, characters, organizations, places, events, and incidents are either product's of the author's imagination or are used fictitiously.

Publisher: Caldera Books
Email: calderabooks@gmail.com

ISBN-13: 978-1539661115
ISBN-10: 1539661113

Cover by Kelly Crimi
Interior book design by Bob Houston eBook Formatting

First Edition (November 1, 2016)

CONTENTS

This book is dedicated to
Francesca, Giovanna, Paola and Donatella
and the cats who adopted them
Dante, Guido, Gattone, Fosca and Pussipu.

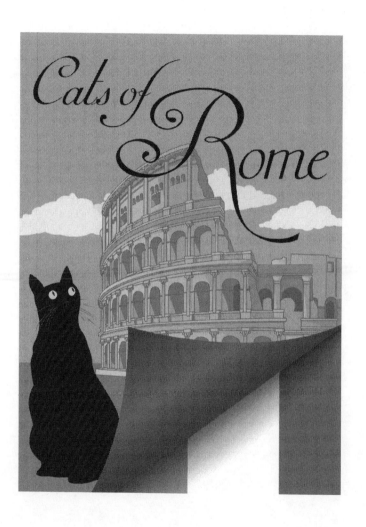

CATS OF ROME:

Flavia, Cicero & Rocco

Dawn crawled down the dozen pitted marble columns in the sunken piazza known as Largo di Torre Argentina. A commotion in the ruined Temple of Juturna woke Cicero, interrupting a dream in which he was about to pounce on a striped lizard. The constant rumble of the Rome city buses and the honking buzz of Vespa scooters twelve feet above the ancient archeological site normally never bothered his sleep. Cicero, an old gray tabby, liked to slumber late in the unseasonably warm January mornings, but a fight between two of his kind made this impossible.

The first thing he noticed was not the identities of the combatants. It was the bad taste in his mouth.

He spit out the beetle leg caught between his right incisors. He wished that he had visited the water trough before falling asleep.

The battle was only verbal, but too close for comfort or a return to sleep. Flavia, a one-eyed Siamese, was in a dispute with Rocco, a big raggedy black and tan tomcat, who had clearly won and lost a number of brawls. This fight didn't come to blows because the two were the best of friends.

"Don't make me come over there to adjudicate," Cicero called. As the colony's elder statesman that job usually fell to him.

He stretched on the top of the carved tomb where he had spent the night, wincing at the pain in his hip joints. The marble lid held the heat of the previous day until long after midnight, he'd discovered. It was preferable to the damp ground under the bushes, stone benches and fallen pillars where most of the other 243 residents of the colony chose to sleep.

"It's not a fight," claimed Rocco, ambling over, ignoring that his twitching stub of a tail gave lie to the words. "Flavia is just spreading rumors that the sanctuary is going to be closed."

"It's not a rumor. It's a certainty," hissed Flavia, her blue eye flashing. "Didn't you see those humans yesterday?" She batted a small plastic water bottle out of her path. "I don't know why the humans throw their trash down on us. Why don't they throw a *panino* or some *trippa*?

"Don't act stupid, Flavia." Rocco retorted. "There are signs all around the square that say, *Don't feed the cats*. But none that read, *Don't litter*."

She came to sit beside him on the path, looking up at Cicero, returning to the subject of the dispute. "Those people were touring the sanctuary buildings with a plan to tear them down."

"I saw them. There are always people here," Rocco answered, taking a quick nip at the flea biting his left flank. "This is where every cat lover in the world comes when they visit Rome. The other day a man said that there are more selfies taken with cats in the background on these ancient ruins than in the Sistine Chapel, whatever that is."

"Tourists don't wear suits and ties. Those were bureaucrats." Flavia spat the words out as if she had eaten a moldy mouse by mistake.

Cicero stretched a paw down the side of the tomb to catch her attention. "Flavia, we are the elite feline colony in the Eternal City. Of course, influential Romans are going to come here. I heard that one of the gentlemen was the mayor."

"That's right, but the ones deciding the fate of the sanctuary were the tubby guy with the wispy hair and the tomato stain on his tie and the lady with bird legs sticking out of a tweedy skirt. I wish I had bitten her on the ankle."

"That wouldn't have helped us much," observed Cicero. "Who was she?"

"Who's more important than the mayor?" said Rocco at the same time.

"She's the *Soprintendente Speciale per i Beni Archeologici di Roma.*"

"Wow, that's a mouthful." Rocco grinned.

"For our situation here in an archeological site, she is more important than the mayor or anybody else, except the Prime Minister."

Cicero understood. "This place is owned by Italy, not Rome. It's considered historic. You know Brutus saved the Republic when he killed Julius Caesar right over…"

"Yeah, yeah, we know. Inside the Curia of Pompey. Stabbed 23 times. You've told us that story a thousand times. There's not even a cat in the whole tale." Flavia stopped, abashed at her own rudeness.

"But the feline sanctuary has been here forever," protested Rocco, oblivious to the historical import of the ruins.

Cicero shook his head. "No, it was started only about 25 years ago. I was one of the first official residents." He paused and clarified, "I mean the human involvement. Of course, there have been cats here for much longer." He winked down at Flavia acknowledging her priorities. "But the clinic, shop and kitchen haven't been here much longer than I have."

"Well, that's going to end," she asserted. "The fat man said the *cat ladies* are occupying one of the most important archeological sites in Torre Argentina, which is *incompatible* with the preservation of the monument – whatever that means." Flavia added emphasis with swooshes of her tail.

Cicero started saying, "I remember when health officials…" before Flavia interrupted, blurting, "More *bureaucrats*."

"… decreed the shelter an 'inappropriate environment' for volunteers and visiting tourists, let alone for the cats," he finished.

"The lady said, 'We're not against cats, but it's our responsibility to protect Italy's archaeological patrimony and to apply the law.' She said our dear ladies were *squatters*. Is that like strays, like us?" Flavia jumped up beside Cicero. "The mayor said 'I'm on the side of the cats and so is my own cat, Certosino.' What kind of name is *Certosino*? Imagine being named after a breed. We could call you Signor Short Hair, instead of Rocco. Or me – Seal Point." She shrugged and passed a paw over her distinctive nose.

"It sounds like they just want to get rid of the *gattare*, the cat ladies," said Cicero.

"But we would *starve* without the ladies," exclaimed Rocco, pacing back and forth. "There aren't enough mice or pigeons in the piazza for all of us. I haven't seen a rat in ages." He stopped and looked toward the sanctuary headquarters under Via Florida at the south end of the square. "By the way, isn't it time for the morning meal?"

"Must be," said Flavia from her perch. "Look, the calico twins are on the move." She pointed her nose at an old pair of sisters, one missing her back right leg. "And the crowd from the Feronia Temple is swarming. We're not going to fit in the first seating."

She almost fell off the tomb when Cicero turned in a quick circle, his tail whipping past her nose. *"What! Watch it!"*

"Did you see that?" He peered down the other side where a broken column with a Roman Doric capital lay. "Rocco, I think we have an eavesdropper."

The tomcat zipped off the path. "It's probably Mimmo. He's always trying to creep up on folks and then pounce on them in a sneak attack. He almost gave me heart failure yesterday."

"Wrong color. Mimmo's an orange tabby," said Cicero. "This is a white ball of fluff. See her, Flavia?"

Flavia turned her head to compensate for her missing eye. "Yes, just the tail. I think it's a stranger." She directed Rocco, "Head down the marble and jump over the end. You'll get her."

Rocco scampered, leaped and captured the spy.

The three cats circled the intruder. She wasn't a kitten, but still young, maybe just over a year old and whiter than any other cat in the colony, a pampered Persian puss.

"Don't scare her, Rocco," said Flavia.

"Scare? Me? I'm a charmer, not a bully." He kept batting at the small cat with the pad of his paw. "She's the one hissing and has needles for claws. She's going to take off the end of my nose."

Cicero cocked his head to one side and rumbled in a low voice, "Bambina, you're safe. But you seem to be lost. This isn't your home."

The white cat didn't answer, but with the agility of youth bounded over Flavia's back to the capital of the fallen column and from there to the top of the tomb. There she paused looking down at the threesome.

"Okay," Flavia said. "Stay up there and we'll talk."

Cicero padded over to the path and lay down, motioning for Rocco to hang back. He nodded at Flavia.

"Let me introduce us," she started. "I'm Flavia. That big, but really nice, guy is Rocco. This grandfather is Cicero." She looked up, her eye wide. "What's your name?"

"Biancaneve," she said a small high voice.

"White Snow? That's a pretty elegant name for a little thing like you."

"Sometimes I'm just called Bianca."

Rocco inched forward, impatient. "Are you new around here?"

"Does that line ever work for you, Rocco?" Flavia turned her back on him. "Of course, you are. We know all of the other 240 felines in the Largo di Torre Argentina. You must have been dropped off. Right? When? Last night? You look too clean to have been here for long."

"Flavia, patience," warned Cicero. "Let me try." He rolled over in the dust, showing his stomach, then rolled back, not looking directly at the elevated cat. "Bambina, where is your home? Did you get locked out by mistake?"

"Nooo," howled Bianca, making them all wince.

Cicero sat up. "Tell me, *tesoro*."

"They *left* me. They don't *want* me anymore."

"Who?"

"My lady and her gentleman friend."

"Start at the beginning, Bianca," prompted Flavia.

"Just over a year ago, at Christmas time …"

"Maybe not that far ba…," Rocco started.

"… my lady's gentleman friend gave me to her as a holiday surprise. I was just a month old." Bianca closed her eyes, smiling at the memory. "She took me everywhere with her in a soft plush velvet bag."

Flavia's eye widened in horror. "Eww."

"But I got too heavy or, at least, that's what she said. She bought me a pillow and put it in the window seat in her bedroom." Bianca looked a little sad at the thought. "Then three weeks ago the gentleman friend brought a Christmas gift – a teacup poodle, a dog tinier than me."

"A *dog*," Rocco said as if he wanted to spit.

"What happened?" Cicero urged.

"She started taking him everywhere with her. He was scared of me, too, even though I tried to be a friend."

"Dogs," Rocco huffed. "Never trust them even the young ones. They may act scared, but then they turn around and bite you in the tuchus." He gave his abbreviated tail a swipe with his tongue.

"You lived in one of the palazzos around here?" Cicero's eyes swept around above the walls of the sunken Torre Argentina square to the overlooking buildings, mostly ancient Renaissance palaces and medieval towers with a few modern additions.

"No, it was somewhere by the Borghese Gardens. We came here by car."

"Why here?" Flavia was perplexed, but Cicero had heard this story before, different details, but the same sad tale.

"My lady and her gentleman friend planned a *settimana bianca*, a ski vacation, in a place called Cortina. Only one of us could go on the plane, they said."

"Why would you want to go on a plane?"

"You don't understand, Rocco," Bianca said, finally comfortable with the big tom. "They said since there was no one to care for me and since there are lots of cats here, it was the best plan to leave me here."

Flavia jumped up on the tomb. Bianca backed up as the Siamese advanced on her. She stopped at the edge. "Are you saying that they went on vacation and just dropped you off to fend for yourself?"

Cicero answered for the frightened cat. "You're too new here, Flavia. They brought you in from the Forum colony because of your eye surgery just five months ago. This kind of thing usually happens at the beginning of summer, not so much in the fall and winter."

"What?" Flavia demanded, turning her back on the relieved Bianca.

"Families go to the beach for a month or more. Before they leave town they abandon their cats at the Torre Argentina sanctuary." Cicero appeared to rub a pain above his eyes away with his paw. "It's either here or at the AutoGrill on the highway to Bibbona or Forte dei Marmi or at the ferry stop to Isola d'Elba. They know that they can get a new cat when they get back."

Flavia was speechless, but Rocco said, "Don't worry, Bianca. You can join our family within the colony. We'll take care of you."

Cicero shook his head as the two females clambered down. "Don't promise that, Rocco. This colony is for disabled and unwell cats." He tried to give Bianca a reassuring look as the foursome cut across the circular temple site, through the sandy orange columns to where breakfast was being served. "The bambina here will have to visit the Director and be checked by the Doctor."

Bianca stopped, but Flavia urged her on. "Don't worry they are both very nice."

"My point is that unlike us, you are one of the lucky ones. You are young, cute and healthy." He licked her ear and bumped her shoulder with his. "My guess is that you will be adopted within a week. And this time it will be a good forever home, not with some silly mean girl."

The building housing the sanctuary clinic, kitchen and offices was probably an illegal shanty in the eyes of the superintendent in charge of Rome's ancient ruins, but to Cicero, who had lived outside of it for most of his 19 years, it was a palace from which only good things came.

He remembered when the floor was a mix of cement and hard-packed earth. Now it was covered with creamy white ceramic tiles. He remembered when three or four ladies carried water down the steps every morning to fill the water bowls. Now there was the magic of water that came out of the walls into basins inside and a hose outside that was used to fill the low water trough for the cat colony.

Years ago when one of his kind needed medical care, they were bundled into a box and carried away, perhaps to return, perhaps not. Now almost all of the ailing cats lived in the clinic in their own tiny enclosures and each of the new residents spent a day there getting tested, vaccinated and what the ladies called *la tecnica della sterilizzazioni*, or "fixed" for short.

Cicero could not remember ever staying in the clinic, except for a few days when he had a bad cough four years before. He was one of the few members of the colony who did not have some physical or mental disability. He was just old and a favorite of all of the ladies. There were now over 25 women and a few men, who had regular shifts at the sanctuary.

Rocco took off at a run toward the wide steps of the ruined teatro where two *gattare*, young and cute in their tight blue jeans and pony tails, were spooning food out of cans onto paper plates and pouring kibble into plastic bowls.

Cicero and Flavia urged Bianca toward the door leading to the clinic and offices, but Cicero stopped when he saw two of his favorite ladies coming down the steps from the street. They both wore the same thing every time he saw them: long black robes, black shoes with thick rubber soles, and a hat that hung around their shoulders, relieved only with a thin white band around their faces. Sister Guadalupe had smooth light brown skin and with a few wisps of straight black hair poking out from her wimple. Sister Agatha's face was all cream and pink with the longest nose Cicero had ever seen on a human and blue eyes that were fading with age.

"Flavia, there are the Sister Ladies," he said, nudging her shoulder. "They'll help with Bianca."

Sure enough. "Cicero, who do you have there?" Sister Agatha squatted down beside the threesome, her hand running from Cicero's nose to the end of his tail. She held out her other hand for Flavia to sniff, knowing that the Siamese needed a moment or two to decide whether she wanted to be touched. Bianca backed up against the wall.

"That's a new one," said Sister Agatha. She sat down on a nearby bench and reached over slowly along the ground, first touching Cicero's paw and then over to the white cat. Bianca sniffed the proffered fingers. They smelled of roses. "I think it's a domestic. Boy or girl, do you think?" Sister Agatha raised her hand to scratch Bianca's ears and the white cat drew back, trying to make herself smaller.

"Try the scratching, patting move," said Sister Guadalupe. "Maybe you can get it up on the bench. They are always less scared when they are higher up."

Sister Agatha ran her fingers over the wooden slates of the bench. All three cats watched from below as she seemed to make lights and shadows dance on the wood with an enticing *scritch scratch* sound. Flavia was the first to leap onto the seat beside the nun and capture the flying fingers. Bianca couldn't seem to stop herself from joining the game. Sister Agatha made her long white fingers scamper across her lap and the white cat followed only to find herself loosely clasped in two warm hands. She froze.

"Definitely a pet. Well fed," her captor said. She was tipped quickly head down and then up. "A little girl. Maybe nine months or a year."

Sister Guadalupe kept petting Cicero, but again put her hand out to Flavia. "She seems to have made a couple of friends, but I don't think she's been here long. Too clean. Abandoned or lost, do you think?"

"I'm going to take her inside." Sister Agatha stood, slowly straightening her long back. "Hopefully the Director is here this morning."

"I'll stay with Cicero and Pirata to give them some love for bringing us this new one."

Flavia looked down at the old cat from her perch on the bench. "Why does she insist on calling me Pirata? Doesn't she know my name by now?"

"The first ladies gave me my name because some guy named Cicero used to speak here back in ancient times. Rocco had a collar with his name on it when he was found. You already had a name, but how were they to know?"

"That kid carried me here from the Forum, half dead from an infection. He knew about the clinic." Flavia patted the space where her missing eye would have been then licked her paw, and smoothed the fur around the scar. "But I still can't understand why they are calling me Pirata."

"Remember that book Beppe had in his back pocket last week. It had a picture of a pirate on the front, a man with a patch over one eye. You look kind of like a cat pirate with one eye. I think it's a compliment. He looked like a very dashing human."

"Flavia's my name."

"To us. Always."

"Let's go find out if we are going to be kicked out of the Torre Argentina. I may not be a pirate, but I am a good undercover operative."

Cicero slunk through the open door and headed toward the Director's office. He and she were old friends and he was one of the few cats who were allowed into her private space. He found the padded basket near the door empty and settled in for a nap. He was a light sleeper and would rouse for any pertinent conversations. The Director was not behind her desk. He thought that she was probably back in the clinic with the two nuns and Bianca.

Flavia also zipped through the door, but she went directly to the sanctuary's store where volunteers sold cat-related toys, mugs, knick-knacks, t-shirts and books. Some were generic, but others were specific to the Torre Argentina Sanctuary, like the book about Nelson, a big white long-haired cat who used to live in the colony. Flavia especially liked this book, written by Deborah, an American volunteer, because Nelson only had one eye, too. Cicero told her, soon after she arrived at the sanctuary, that when he was a youngster he knew Nelson, the king cat of the colony. He was long dead, having spent his last days in a home in a place called Germany. Now Cicero was the elder statesman of the cat tribe.

The store wasn't open for business, but Flavia knew that the best gossips among the lady volunteers worked the cash register and stocked the shelves. If there were news to be had from the humans, she would hear it there first. She tucked herself away in a basket of furry fake cats. Many times in the past she had fooled the tourists shopping for "a little something" to take home to a grandchild.

Rocco was on his third course, having nibbled on chicken bits, followed by some tuna. He liked to finish with a bit of dry kibble to clean his teeth, but stopped chewing to listen to one of the volunteers.

"My mother said the Director is calling a meeting to get the word out." Pammy, the daughter of the U.S. ambassador, was picking up the empty paper food bowls and throwing them into an extra-large garbage bag. "Can you imagine what a zoo it's going to be when all of the cat ladies and their kids and grandkids start marching around the perimeter of Largo di Torre Argentina." She was talking to a Dutch schoolmate from the International School. They volunteered two mornings a week before classes started. Both were getting extra credit for "social awareness."

"Maybe if we offer to make posters and write letters to members of Parliament, we can use this for our government class project," said Maj, reaching up to scratch the ruff of an orange tabby on the step above where she was sweeping. "How are you feeling today, Buttercup? Did the doctor clear out the mites in your ears?" She peered into the cat's left ear.

Rocco went back to munching the dry food, fearing Pammy was going to slip it out from beneath his nose.

"Eww, I don't know how you can deal with the bug stuff," said Pammy, rolling the rubber gloves a little further up her slender arms.

Maj laughed. "It all washes off. Anyway, her ears got dosed two days ago. I helped."

"I'm fine with the ones that have had their baths and are in the cages inside and I love to just sit and watch the antics out here, but I'm never going to be a vet, like you."

"Just an assistant veterinarian, right now. But when I get back home next year, I'll start my training." Maj finished sweeping behind Pammy. The next feeding would take place on the steps in the evening. "So how serious is this eviction thing?"

Rocco perked up his ears and Pammy grabbed the empty plastic bowl from under his chin. "Rocco, I saw you on the lower step five minutes ago. Did you miss dinner last night or are you just being *goloso*?" She picked up three more bowls and turned to Maj. "It must be serious. My mother said it all started when the Director put in a request to the proper authorities for permission to put in a toilet and hook the drains up to the sewage system."

"A toilet? Wouldn't that be fabulous?" Maj swept the last of the remnants of the morning meal in to a dustpan and dumped it into Pammy's plastic bag. "I never get coffee before I come here because I don't want to use the facilities at the café across the street."

"You are so totally right." Pammy shuddered at the thought. "Anyway, Mother said that it was when the planning people came to inspect the sanctuary headquarters that the trouble started. I guess most of the place was built into a cave under Via Florida without permission."

"I suppose that sewer pipes couldn't be snuck in overnight." Maj gave Rocco a quick rubdown since he seemed to be asking for it with his steady stare. "Rocco, make sure you drink a lot of water, today," she said. "With all that food you don't want to get constipated."

"Eww," groaned Pammy. "TMI, Maj! Way too much info."

The two friends headed to the food preparation room to wash up and finish their shift. Rocco padded over to the long, low water trough. He wondered why Cicero and Flavia had decided to skip the morning meal. He'd keep an eye out for a couple of mice in case they got a little peckish.

Cicero woke as the Director rushed into the office while trying to dig her *telefonino* out of her capacious woven leather satchel.

"Doctor, see if that new one has a microchip. I've got to get this," she called over her shoulder. She found the cell phone and punched the screen. "*Pronto.*" She listened for a minute and then said in Italian, "I'm so glad you called. We are trying to get articles in all of the papers and in the weekly magazines, too." She was quiet again for a bit and then said, "I would be happy to give an interview and to take your photographer on a tour of the facility and the ruins. Evening is the best time for photographing cats in the *piazza.*"

Cicero stretched and jumped first to the visitor chair and then to the top of the desk. The Director, an elegant woman with long gray hair braided in an intricate knot at the back of her head, ran her long arthritic fingers through Cicero's fur. The person on the other end of the phone call finally quit talking.

"That's correct. The mayor is on our side, but he has no say in the matter. But a number of members of Parliament have called to offer their support. If you remember – over ten years ago – the Rome City Council recognized the Torre Argentina feline colony's historical bond with the city and declared it, as well as the cats at the ruins at the Coliseum and Forum, as part of the City's *bio-cultural heritage*," she said with emphasis, then waited for a response. "Yes, you should be able to find articles about that in the paper's archives. Or just Google it."

The Director listened some more and then hung up after saying, "I will look forward to meeting you this afternoon at four." She sat, quietly massaging Cicero's aching hips for a couple of minutes and then called through the open door. "Lucia and Marco, do you think we can get a crowd down here with some signs this afternoon?"

Flavia heard the last bit through the door of the store as Sister Guadalupe and Sister Agatha entered, coming from the infirmary where they had fed the caged post-operative and ailing cats.

"We see you there, Pirata," Sister Agatha said to Flavia with a giggle. "You keep trying to hide from us, but you haven't quite perfected the look of a stuffed toy. Most of them have two eyes. Maybe if you tried lying on your side."

"Leave her some pride, Agatha. She tries so hard to fool us." She unlocked the cash register. "Or maybe she's only hiding from the visitors."

Flavia ignored them, feigning a nap.

"I'm going to start sorting the postcards and the calendars," the young nun said.

If Flavia had hoped for gossip about the potential closure of the sanctuary, she was disappointed. The two started chatting about the state of the garden – excellent according to them – at a place called "The Vatican" and although it seemed like an ideal spot for cats to live there were reportedly none in residence.

"I'm thinking of adding to the kitchen garden," said Sister Guadalupe. "It would be so helpful to have a wider variety of herbs, especially for the Argentinian dishes. Some cilantro, lemon basil, a variety of hot peppers, and a spicy parsley or, at least, more spicy than Italian parsley. Do you think we can plant some Crocus for saffron or is it too late?"

"Guadalupe, you know I have no understanding about plants. I kill them just by looking at them. Excuse me for changing the subject, but did you hear the Director say that we should leave early so as to not get mixed up in some demonstration about the *gattile*."

"Yes, I think we should leave by noon," said her friend.

"I told the Director that we would take a bunch of the cat blankets and beds back with us to launder using our big washing machines." She looked up as a couple of American tourists, decked out in shorts and flip-flops, came in to shop. *Hardly the garb for even a warm January morning*, thought Sister Agatha.

The pudgy man said, "Hello, Sister! We hear there is a book about a one-eyed cat called Nelson, named for the British war hero."

She turned to the bookshelves. "Here it is. We only have one left."

"Lucky we are," said the wife. "We're planning to make a sizable gift to the sanctuary. Too hard to take a cat home, but we will feel like we've helped. We rented a place across Corso Vittorio Emanuele and have come here every day for a week in between the museums and the ruins. That way we didn't miss our three cats at home in Omaha so much."

"I understand," said Sister Guadalupe. "When I came here from Argentina, I had to leave my two old cats at my convent in Córdoba."

"So you're a friend of the Pope," said the American woman at the same time her husband said, "You're from Argentina and this is Torre Argentina. Funny coincidence."

The nun responded to her first. "I knew His Holiness's sister and she suggested that I come to Rome to supervise his kitchen." Then, to the man she said, "Actually Torre Argentina has nothing to do with the South American country. It was named for a tower – *torre* – that takes its name from the city of Strasbourg, of all things, whose Latin name was *Argentoratum*. In 1503, the Papal Master of Ceremonies Johannes Burckardt, who came from

Strasbourg was known as *Argentinus*. He built a palace in Via del Sudario – you can find it at number 44 – called Casa del Burcardo. The tower was part of the palace."

"My goodness, Sister," he said, scratching his bald head. "We learned more this morning than we have all week. Our apartment is right near the intersection with Via del Sudario. Now we'll go find that tower you mentioned and get a photo of Colleen and me in front of it."

Sister Agatha, not to be outdone with neighborhood trivia, piped up, "You won't find the tower any more. It was incorporated into the palazzo. But if you want to see a real tower find the Torre del Papito. It's at the corner between Via Florida and Via di S. Nicola de' Cesarini, just above us, here. The origin of the name Papito is uncertain, but some believe that it comes from the antipope Anacleto II Pierleoni, nicknamed *Papetto* or *Papito* due to his short height."

"What's an antipope?" asked the woman from Nebraska.

Sister Guadalupe winked at Sister Agatha, knowing that she had gotten herself into a muddle.

Sister Agatha grimaced and answered, "It's complicated. Back in the 1100s there were two competing popes, chosen by two different sets of cardinals. That said, it would never happen today."

By this point Flavia had had enough. She slipped out of the pile of stuffed cats, causing the man to drop his wallet in surprise. She had an idea. She needed to find Cicero and Rocco.

After sticking her nose into the Director's office and failing to catch a whiff of Cicero, Flavia headed outdoors to the watering station where she found both of her friends. Rocco was sitting on the pedestal near the faucet keeping an eye on a quartet of kittens harassing a live cricket. Cicero was making up for missing breakfast by filling his stomach with water.

Flavia lapped up water until one of the kittens tripped over her tail. She hissed at all four, sending them scurrying for safety up the trunk of an ancient wisteria vine that wound its way up the wall beside the sanctuary headquarters.

"Okay, you two," she said to Rocco and Cicero. "I have a plan. Unless you learned something different since we split up, I think we need to be ready to move to a new home whenever the bureaucrats come to evict us."

Cicero scrunched his brow. "Flavia, I think you are being too hasty. There is nothing that says that the colony is going to be moved. Just the building."

"But if the building goes, the ladies go, and if the ladies go then the food goes," moaned Rocco. "Is there food in this alternative home?" He jumped down and planted himself in front of Flavia, staring at her one eye as if to verify her trustworthiness.

"I know there is a garden. Where there is a garden, there are at least mice and voles and probably birds." Flavia saved the best news for last. "And the garden belongs to Sister Guadalupe. She'll feed us. I heard she has a kitchen so there will be scraps and she'll probably even bring us the food we like best. She knows what it is."

"But how do we get there?" Cicero seemed less concerned now that there would be a familiar human around. "We don't know where Sister Guadalupe and Sister Agatha live. We only know that they always arrive here together."

Rocco started to do an odd little dance. "I know. I know," he chattered as if a tasty bird were just inches away. "I was up on top by the street. They came in a car. I've seen them before. They always leave it near the stairs. They'll take us to their garden."

"No they won't, Rocco." Flavia batted his nose with a paw. "But you are partly right. We will go with them, but on the sly. They won't know that we are there."

Rocco looked confused. Cicero looked concerned. "How do you plan to do this, Flavia?" the old cat asked.

"I heard Sister Agatha say that they were to take a load of the blankets and beds from inside to their home," Flavia explained. "We will watch as they carry them up to their car and will slip in when they open the door. You know we are good at slipping in places. We'll hide under the blankets."

Cicero thought for a moment. "I guess that is safe enough. If they discover us, they will just bring us back to Torre Argentina. They aren't going to abandon us somewhere dangerous."

"Right," urged Flavia. "This is only a mission to discover if there is an alternative to these ruins for us and our friends. We'll want to come back and get the others." She didn't really mean this, but she knew Cicero was attached to the colony, having been its leader since old one-eyed Nelson died.

Rocco was good at logistics. "I think Cicero needs to sit up on the top step near the street gate because he isn't so fast anymore. I'll watch the Sister ladies from the ledge by the window of the store and let you both know when they start gathering up the blankets. Flavia will take a position at the bottom of the stairs just in case I get a bit distracted and miss them carrying things out to their car."

Flavia nodded. "Once we are all at the top, we will hope they have to come down again for more bedding and we'll hop in and burrow under the laundry. If they only make one trip we will have to be extra sneaky."

"The only hope we have is that they are so used to cats on the steps that they won't notice we are close to the car," said Cicero. "Maybe one of you can be a distraction."

The plan worked pretty well – not perfect, but pretty well.

As Sister Agatha came up the marble stairs to the street, Cicero tucked himself halfway under the hem of her habit, even though it meant her heels knocked his nose once or twice. He lucked out when she left the hatchback of the Fiat 500 open after she put a pile of filthy cat beds in the back and then turned to call down the stairs, "Guadalupe, do you need me to come down and help you with the rest?"

Cicero levered up using the rear bumper and tucked himself under the beds. Seconds later Flavia joined him. "Where's Rocco?" he murmured in her ear.

"He was coming up the stairs in front of Sister Guadalupe, but he's so big I'm not sure how he's going to stay out of sight."

Sister Agatha opened the driver's side door, but stopped as she started to get in. "Just a minute, you're dragging a blanket. Let me help you." The two layered the rest of the laundry in the back of the small car.

Rocco still hadn't joined them.

"Hey you! Get out of there," Sister Agatha yelled.

Sister Guadalupe slammed the hatchback and peered around at her friend. "What happened?"

"A cat on my seat," she laughed. "I wonder how its driving would have been."

"It didn't run under the car did it?"

"No, back down the stairs. Never fear." Sister Agatha got in as her friend opened the passenger door. "What a smell. It's certainly past the time for washing those beds."

"Agatha, that was the start of this whole mess. If the Director hadn't wanted to install a toilet and a washing machine, she probably wouldn't have the planning commission and thereafter, the *Beni Archeologici di Roma* down on her neck."

The small car pulled out into traffic, resulting in the blare of the horn of a city bus.

"Watch out. I think I'm going to have to get my driver's license. I haven't had time since arriving from Argentina last June, but you are getting a bit absentminded."

Agatha took the corner onto Via Florida at speed. "Not at all. I've always driven like this. In Rome it's the only way to drive – offensively, not defensively." She pressed down on the accelerator as if to emphasize her point.

The next hard left flung Flavia into the side of the car out from under the blankets. She stuck her head up to see a Vespa driven by a being hidden behind the dark gray visor of a black helmet come within inches of the hatchback's window before it veered to the right and roared past. She dove under the pile of wash straight into Cicero's stomach.

"Umf," he blew out. "Careful, Bambina."

"There are monsters out there," she mewed.

"Don't let them see you."

"I thought I smelled Rocco."

"Wishful thinking. Anyway there are the odors of a thousand cats around us. How you could smell him, I can't imagine."

The car shimmied again. The two nauseous cats went silent.

"Have you visited Chiesa del Gesù?" Sister Agatha shift down to slow for a Ford Focus with a Hertz Rental sticker on the bumper. "Tourists," she muttered.

"Is that the one we just passed?"

Sister Agatha nodded. "It's the mother church of the Jesuits and you probably don't know that its full name is *Chiesa del Santissimo Nome di Gesù all'Argentina.*"

"Why 'Argentina'?" Sister Guadalupe made air quotes with her fingers.

"I don't know. It was built on the orders of a Spanish cardinal back in the 1500s, and has the first baroque façade, but I don't know what is meant by the name." She turned onto Corso Vittorio Emanuele II, a straight shot to Castel Sant'Angelo, and picked up speed. "I've been inside a couple of times. It's very ornate, something I don't always think fits the Jesuits."

"I think that's where His Holiness said mass a couple of weeks ago. I wasn't there."

"Of course, he would, being a Jesuit himself."

"Agatha, open your window. The smell and your driving are making me positively bilious."

"Hang on there, young thing. We are almost at the bridge." Agatha swung over two lanes. "We'll be out in the garden in a couple of minutes."

After stopping at a guarded gate, the two women drove along a narrow road beside a high ancient wall. "I plan to park outside the laundry," said Sister Agatha. "You can walk across the garden to the kitchen. I'll stay and start the washing machines."

"Remember to do an extra rinse cycle after washing the blankets. We don't want cat hair in His Holiness's cassocks." Sister Guadalupe giggled as she got out of the car. Her friend opened the driver's side door and then reached over to unplug her cell phone from under the dashboard.

It took two trips to carry all of the bedding past the clotheslines into the laundry room, giving Cicero and Flavia a chance to slip out of the open hatchback and under the car. They were not alone.

"What took you so long?" Rocco licked a paw and smoothed it over a raggedy ear.

Flavia was slack jawed. "When? What? How?"

"That stupid youngster, Pepito – you know the one who wants to join the colony and always hangs out by the stairs – distracted Sister Agatha by jumping onto the front seat. When she removed him, I slipped onto the floor in the back and squeezed under the seat. Good thing I'm such a limber guy."

Cicero flattened himself behind a tire. "Quiet! She's coming back."

Sister Guadalupe took her satchel from where she had left it on the hood of the car, slung it across her chest and set off along a path of crushed stone. She ran her hands along the lavender bushes that bordered the walkway, grabbing a sprig to tuck over her ear inside her wimple.

The three cats followed on the outside of the low hedge. Rocco kept up a commentary from the rear. "Nice place. Lots of olive trees over there. Bunches of birds. Bet there're lizards and voles and mice galore. Much cleaner than the sanctuary. Not a whiff of dog. Or cat either. Must be a stable somewhere though."

"Pipe down, Rocco," Flavia muttered. "You want to get us caught."

The danger of discovery was heightened when the hedges ended and the nun turned left through a grove of olive trees. The cats held back, trying to use the trunks as cover without losing sight of the only person they knew in the garden.

Sister Guadalupe went through a tall arched bower of twisted wisteria vines, just beginning to show early spring greenery, into a flower garden. Daffodils, irises, tulips and hyacinths were starting to bud, but no flowers had bloomed. The nun was so intent on looking for the first blossom, she didn't notice the man sitting on a bench tucked behind a small burbling fountain. He rose, slipping a small book in the pocket of his white hassock.

"Your Holiness!" Sister Guadalupe genuflected, and kissed the ring on the hand he held out, before continuing. "I didn't see you there. I'm sorry to disturb. I'll leave." The little flower garden adjoined the kitchen garden. It was not the place she expected to find Pope Francis.

"Be at peace, Sister. I just noticed that it was almost time for the mid-day meal. I'm dining with the new archbishop of Havana. I guess he is somewhat of a cook. He's preparing Cuban delicacies for us."

"So I was informed, Your Holiness," said Sister Guadalupe with a sniff. "Cardinal Parolin sent word that you would not need me until *cena* this evening at eight thirty."

"Something soothing please, Sister," Pope Francis said, looking over her shoulder. "Who knows what kinds of peppers Archbishop Juan García will use." He paused. "Sister, do you have some new friends?"

Sister Guadalupe followed his gaze to where a stubby black and tan tail stuck out from under a low marble bench. "It can't be," she murmured, but then she saw the green eyes of an old gray tabby peering out from a lilac bush that hadn't started to bud. "Not exactly friends, but I do know them."

"Odd looking housecats," he said, sitting back down on the bench and reaching a hand out to Cicero. "I think there is another in the lilac, but I can only see one eye."

"That old one is Cicero. The raggedy guy is Rocco." She squatted to peer under the bush. "And the Siamese is Pirata. Because of the one eye." She looked around. "I surely hope there aren't any more."

"If not housecats, then what, Sister Guadalupe?"

Cicero was drawn to the man for a reason beyond his ken. The Pope scratched that eternal itch between his ears. He purred for the first time in months, which surprised even him. The pontiff felt the vibration and said, "I always liked the saying of Cicero, the philosopher, 'If you have a garden and a library, you have everything you need.' It seems this Cicero just needs a garden."

Rocco threw caution away and advanced down the path. The nun, he knew, was not a threat, and the man with the nice face and glasses, clearly knew how to approach a cat. Sister Guadalupe herded him to the side. "Your Holiness, I hate to say that there may be … umm … fleas. These are residents of the Torre Argentina Sanctuary."

The Pope did not seem disturbed by this news, merely curious. "So how did they come to visit us?"

"My guess is that they caught a ride with Sister Agatha and me."

"But why?"

"I have no clue. The cats have a good life there. The garden may not be so green, but they seem content." The nun kept an eye on Flavia, who was slinking along behind the bench on which the Vicar of Christ sat. "Actually, the only problem lately has been for the volunteers. You may have read that the *Soprintendenza Speciale per i Beni Archeologici di Roma* …"

"A title longer than any of mine …"

"True, Your Holiness," she said with a smile. "Well, she has targeted the sanctuary building under

Via Florida for demolition because no permits were issued when it was built."

"That means the cats won't be fed?"

"Probably not that drastic. Volunteers would always bring food for the colony. But there is a very effective TNR program ..." She paused at the look on his face. "Trap Neuter Release, I mean. It is a way to humanely limit the number of feral cats in the city. The clinic would be destroyed. It would severely limit that effort."

"You are a regular volunteer at Torre Argentina?"

"Yes, Sister Agatha and I are at the sanctuary two half days a week."

Pope Francis nodded. "This requires some thought." He closed his eyes and folded his hands in his lap. Sister Guadalupe sat on the edge of the fountain, her hand firmly on Rocco's back.

"What's he doing?" whispered Flavia from below the bench.

Rocco peered up at the Pope. "Nothing."

"He's praying," said Cicero, tucking his paws under his chest and closing his eyes, a feline replica of the man sitting above him.

The Pope stood and folded his hands inside the sleeves of cassock.

"Do you know what tomorrow is, Sister?"

The next day, January 17, was the feast day of St. Anthony the Abbot, the patron saint of domestic animals. It was the day that the residents of Rome brought their dogs and cats and bunnies and hamsters to Vatican Square where Cardinal-Deacon Comastri blessed the pets in the saint's name.

The afternoon before, Pope Francis asked Sister Guadalupe to gather up her feline "friends" and keep them in the kitchen garden. "Unfortunately, although I would love to have a cat or two around, we cannot have a colony take up residence in the Vatican gardens," he said. "Tomorrow we will take them to their home and maybe we can secure their future."

Flavia was still grumbling that the humans were calling her Pirata rather than by her own name, but that didn't stop her from dining on a can of tuna and sleeping for hours behind a row of fragrant basil plants in the kitchen garden.

She woke at midnight to stroll through the Vatican's formal Italianate garden under a waning moon. She rolled in the soft sweet-smelling grass, used a tall cypress tree as a scratching post, and sipped water from a gurgling spring under the gaze of a ceramic Madonna. She reminded herself that Largo di Torre Argentina had a patch of grass and two cypress trees and a trough of fresh water. Maybe having 242 neighbors didn't provide the magic of a private garden, but it was home.

Rocco curled up near Cicero in an annex to the kitchen, sleeping on an old blanket in the warmth of the house. The novelty of snoozing through a night without having to keep one ear cocked for the stealthy sounds of danger enticed them away from exploring a realm that would never be theirs.

"Let Flavia dream the impossible dream," said Rocco. "She's young."

The next morning, after a proper breakfast, they each tolerated a thorough combing by Sister Agatha before the sound of a vehicle crunched across the gravel near the kitchen's delivery door. Sister Guadalupe picked up Cicero and both Flavia and Rocco felt the need to follow their friend.

"I knew we weren't going to be allowed to stay," Flavia muttered. "It was way too good to be true."

Cicero looked down at her from the nun's arms. "Hush, Flavia. The goal was to make something happen to save the sanctuary. It may not work, but we tried."

In the small courtyard behind the kitchen stood a white Mercedes jeep convertible with a tall glassed-in rear seat area, the Popemobile.

Sister Guadalupe placed Cicero on the white seat beside Pope Francis. Cardinal Parolin scooted closer to the door making more space between his black cassock and the cat, only to be frustrated when Flavia and Rocco joined their friend between the two men. The two nuns climbed up on the front seat with Sabastian Gonzales, the Pope's driver.

As they drove out past the kitchen garden, two horses ridden by Swiss Lancers in their armor and multicolored silks fell in line in front of the popemobile.

"I told you there was a stable," Rocco bragged. "Can't get nothing past this nose."

A black SUV full of men in black suits pulled in behind. The short caravan made its way out from behind the Vatican walls to circle the square in front of St. Peter's Cathedral where a crowd of pet owners had come to receive a blessing from Cardinal-Deacon Comastri, resplendent in his black simar with its red piping and buttons. A red silk sash blew in the January breeze. Next to him stood the mayor, bedecked with a red, white and green sash across the chest of his blue suit, holding his gray, orange-eyed cat Certosino. Neither of them seemed very patient as the Cardinal-Deacon gave a prolonged blessing and sprinkled those gathered with holy water.

Leashed dogs barked. Cats in carry cases or clutched against shoulders dug their claws in and wished they were home. A few horses and a couple of ponies were munching on hay in the corner of the square. Behind the central dais was a long row of cages holding pet goats, rabbits, poultry and a ewe with lambs.

The unannounced appearance of Pope Francis sent a cheer up through the gathering. The people moved to follow his slow progress out of the piazza, around the Castel Sant'Angelo and across the Tiber on the Ponte Sant'Angelo. A full cadre of black-suited guards now walked beside the Pope as he stood at the roll-bar behind the glass and waved to the people rushing to line the streets. The three cats vacillated between excitement and fear in the face of the teeming crowds, but the slow speed of progress at least allowed them to keep their seats.

That is until Rocco, following for the first time the universal law that dictates that cats are drawn to any human who dislikes them, crawled into Cardinal Parolin's lap and poked his head out the side of the popemobile in order to see the great river below. One of the men in black gave him a quick scratch between the ears. The Cardinal sat petrified.

Too soon (except for Cardinal Parolin) the cavalcade arrived at Largo di Torre Argentina. As they approached the sanctuary, a big van with a satellite dish on top swerved in behind the black SUV.

Pope Francis stepped out of his transport and, followed by Flavia, Cicero and Rocco, he made his way down the marble stairs into the ancient ruins. Cats ran from all corners of the archeological site to see what was going on, while still keeping a safe distance. The Director, who had been warned by Sister Guadalupe to expect His Holiness, was waiting outside the door of the sanctuary building, dressed in a green linen dress covered by a blue smock with *Colonia Felina Torre Argentina* embroidered across the back and in tiny script on the breast pocket. She genuflected and when he held a hand out to urge her to stand, she kissed the pontiff's ring. Cicero stood at her feet.

"Your elder statesman," the Pope said, pointing at the gray tabby, "asked me to come and see what I can do to assist you."

"Your Holiness, we are honored by your presence on this the feast day of St. Anthony the Abbot." The Director was aware of the television camera behind the pontiff. "We believe that if the citizens of Rome knew that we were in danger of being evicted – not the cats, but those who feed and care for them – then maybe some other solution could be found."

"Perhaps you would be so kind as to give me a tour of your facilities." The Pope turned to follow the Director inside. Cardinal Parolin followed him, with Sister Agatha and Sister Guadalupe bringing up the rear. Cicero and Flavia joined the tour group by using the Pope's hassock as cover. The men in black blocked the cameraman from entering and soon all of the morning volunteers blocked the entrance trying to get a glimpse of the Pope. Rocco sat on the windowsill of the clinic and could see quite nicely.

The tour ended in the clinic where the Director introduced the veterinarian and explained the program, which cared for injured and sick felines, as well as limited the future population growth of Rome's feral cats. Young Bianca was held as an example of a cat who would soon be placed up for adoption into a forever home. The three blind calico kittens sleeping in one of the clinic cages would probably have to join the colony, the Director said.

Flavia and Cicero climbed the pyramid of cages to join Bianca in a kitty bed on the top.

"You're famous, Bambina," said Cicero. "The doctor was filming you with her phone. I heard her say she was going to put it on something called YouTube."

"Maybe my lady will see me and decide to bring me home."

Flavia shook her head. "You don't want to go back there. You can do better."

As the small group left the clinic, the Pope then asked to see the ruins of the Teatro Pompeo, the theater complex that had once covered the entire Torre Argentina site when it was completed in 55BC. Luisa, one of the older volunteers, had spent years studying the history of Pompey the Great, who ordered the theater built, and later the Orsini family, which had used the ancient stones to build a family fortress. She led the tour, urged by the Director to provide "only the highlights."

Most of the cats in the colony had just finished their post-breakfast baths so they staked out spots to watch the tour from atop tombs, stairs and fallen pillars. The television crew tried to keep at least one cat in every shot of the Pope.

When the pontiff came to the steps in the Curia of Pompey where Julius Caesar met his fate, he paused at the top and turned to the crowd of sanctuary volunteers. He raised his voice to be heard by the people packed along the railings far above, and said:

"Blessed are you, O Lord, who for the sake of our comfort gave us domestic animals as companions. The animals of God's creation inhabit the skies, the earth and the sea. They share the fortunes of human existence and have a part in human life. God, who confers his gift on all living things, has often used the service of animals or made them symbolic reminders of the gifts of salvation. Animals were saved from the flood and afterwards made part of the covenant with Noah. The paschal lamb brings deliverance from the bondage of Egypt; a giant fish saved Jonah; ravens brought bread to Elijah; animals were included in the repentance enjoined on humans."

He paused for a moment and then added, "And animals shared in Christ's redemption of all God's creation. We therefore invoke the divine blessing on these animals through the intercession of Saint Anthony the Abbot. As we do, let us praise the Creator and thank him for giving mankind the responsibility and care for all of the other creatures of the earth, including the cats of Torre Argentina."

As he stepped down among the volunteers he said to the Director, "I think I can help more with a concrete act today. May I adopt that small white cat when she is ready to leave the clinic?"

"Of course, Your Holiness."

"I will call her Chiara, which means clear light and fits her white beauty, and is also the name of the sainted woman who helped Saint Francis in his ministry."

Cicero heard this and smiled to himself. All would be well for Bianca (or Chiara, now), in her forever home. It fit with his philosophy of an ultimately just world.

"I think the three blind kittens might cause too much havoc among the stiff and proper members of my staff, but I think Sister Guadalupe would welcome them into her kitchen garden. Perhaps the Vatican carpenters can create a small *gattile* for them. What do you think, Sister?"

The nun was pink with pleasure. "Your Holiness, I would be so happy to give them a home. I always wanted a cat or two," she glanced quickly at Cardinal Parolin's pinched face, "but was told that that would not be possible."

"Some rules are meant to be broken," said the Pope with a grin before growing serious. "You know that Cicero – the ancient man, not the cat – once said: 'The higher we are placed, the more humbly we should walk.' Probably our old feline friend knows that, too." He bent to run his hand down the gray cat's boney spine.

As Pope Francis climbed the stairs to the popemobile, he turned and called out, "Sisters, your ride is leaving." He climbed in behind Cardinal Parolin as a blue-suited man with a tri-color sash pushed through the crowd. The mayor arrived after taking Certosino home from the festival at St. Peter's.

Lucky for him the television crew wanted to continue filming. He sat with the Director among the rose-orange columns in the circular *Teatro Fortuna Huiusce Diei*, which meant Fortune of This Day. There they planned for the saving of the Torre Argentina cat sanctuary. Rocco sat in the mayor's lap. Flavia lay at his feet. Cicero looked on from the top of his favorite tomb.

The mayor went home with a warm feeling, good publicity and a number of fleas. And so the Cat Sanctuary at Largo di Torre Argentina was saved and remains active even today.

CATS OF VENICE:

Regina, Fosca & Casanova

Regina's growing displeasure at her lady-in-waiting's failure to serve her afternoon saucer of milk and platter of liver paté was evident in the unblinking concentration of her narrowed slate-blue eyes. The courtier, who was the focus of the penetrating gaze, blithely potted a ficus. Enthroned on a jewel-toned painted dais, spanning the corner of the roof-top terrace fence, Regina contemplated how she would mete out dire consequences. She ignored the fact that the repotting of the plant was largely her fault.

A seagull, as white as Regina herself, gliding on the updraft from the canal, banked toward the small canopy shading Regina, causing her to lose her train of thought and interrupted the transmission of her demand. She followed the bird's flight toward Piazza San Marco with its cathedral and *campanile*, the grand bell tower. For a moment she thought wistfully about the bird's complete freedom as opposed to her imprisonment, but then she realized that Signor Seagull had to forage for his dinner. Regina's was delivered on hand-made Murano glass by a servant, despite human inefficiencies.

"Oh my, your majesty, it's late," said the lady-in-waiting, known by others as Paola. "I was so wrapped up in saving this poor little tree that I forgot your afternoon snack."

She dusted her hands on her potting smock while getting to her feet. "Let me give him a sip or two and we'll go down." Water gurgled through the complex piping system, resulted in a fine spray over the tiny ficus.

Regina turned from contemplating the Byzantine domes of San Marco to look at the shrub in the shower. She would never admit that the shattered pot and dirt all over the living room floor was the result of a wild tarantella she danced with a feather at the end of the long wand. Her jester had rightly taken the blame.

Sliding into her favorite yoga pose – downward cat with a question (her silky plumed tail providing the punctuation) – Regina stretched before stepping off her stage onto the weathered teak railing that bordered the two-level terrace. The Turkish Angora breeding, often called the ballerina of cats, famed for long legs, showed in her every step.

The only tricky part of her elegant balancing act toward the stairs down into the palazzo was at the second to last corner. There Paola maintained a multi-level display of all of her cacti, gathered in hot, dry countries from throughout the world. Paola's failure to change the configuration, even though she always said, "Careful there" every time Regina passed the spot, was another of the lady-in-waiting's failings.

Queens don't have to be careful, *thought Regina*. It's your job to take care of me.

She scampered down two spiral staircases, marched over to her private dining table – a slab of inlaid wood polished to a high sheen – and sat staring at Paola as she removed the dusty blue smock and placed Regina's bowl on the counter.

As Paola opened the refrigerator, the apartment front door slammed open. "Mamma, *sono io.*"

As if there could be any doubt that it was him? *Regina closed her eyes in frustration.*

A boy with light cherubic curls whirled into the kitchen, shedding sweater, scarf, backpack, and shoes. Regina's court jester, Giulio, was home from school.

"*Amore*, how was class today?" Paola set the blue glass bowl on Regina's dining table. The bowl was empty.

My court is in disarray, *fumed Regina.*

"Mamma, guess what… ?"

"Did you finish your report on the effect of cruise ships on the *laguna*?" Paola cut in as she handed him his slippers. Venetian kids did not wear shoes in the house or go barefoot.

"Almost. Signora Zeno wants me to do some research online before I draw my conclusions." He slipped on the rubber-soled woolen shoes and popped up on to a high kitchen stool. "There's a UNESCO site that summarizes the scientific studies. … But more important, I've been asked to be part of the school's dragon boat team for the *Regata Storica* next week."

"*Incredibile*, Giulio!" Paola sounded both happy and alarmed. "I would have thought you were too young and … uh … small to be on a rowing crew."

"*Mamma!*" he protested. "First, there are *paddlers* on a dragon boat, not rowers. And, don't worry, I'm not a paddler or a steerer. I'm the drummer."

"The drummer?"

"Yes, the drummer has to be small and have really, really good rhythm," he grinned and changed the subject. "Can I have Nutella and banana on a slice of bread?"

"Of course, *tesoro*." Paola opened the refrigerator to find the chocolate spread. "Give me half of one of those bananas on the table."

Giulio reached for the platter of fruit. "Regina, what *are* you doing? Mamma, watch out! Regina is rolling her milk bowl under your feet."

"Regina! What are you… ?" She saw the plastic milk bottle on the counter. "Sorry, *gattina*, I forgot to pour your milk."

And you forgot my liver paté. What's milk without liver. Incompetents! Regina yelled, which sounded like caterwauling to her audience. *What did it take to make humans understand the simplest things?* Her elegant tail whipped back and forth horizontally, emphasizing her opinion.

"She's angry at you, Mamma," Giulio said, grinning. "You're going to have to give her extra today."

Paola was pouring the milk when the apartment front door opened again.

"Is that you, Domenico?" "Papà, you're early!" Paola and Giulio spoke at the same time.

The man, who Regina thought of as her footman, entered the kitchen, shedding his jacket.

"Shoes off, darling, " Paola said. "Your mother taught you better than that."

"Papà, I'm going to be the drummer on a dragon boat in next week's *Regata Storica*."

Domenico, a short man with salt and pepper curls and twinkling brown eyes, a much older replica of his son, ruffled Giulio's hair, saying "I can't wait to hear about your team, Giulio" as he headed back out the kitchen door. "Forgot my slippers in the bathroom." He took the stairs to the second floor. "I'll just be a second."

The other thing he had forgotten was to close the front door to the apartment.

Time to teach them who is the queen around here, thought Regina as she squeezed past the heavy door onto the hall landing. She sat behind the umbrella stand. *Let's see how long it takes them to miss me.*

It took longer than she thought it would. She fell asleep behind the umbrellas. When she awoke, the door was shut. She could have scratched at it and yowled – her voice was loud – but she was so incensed she decided to teach her courtiers a lesson.

Two flights down, she paused at the Morosini's apartment door to torment their Welsh terrier, Bruno. Once the dog was in a frenzy, she scurried down two more sets of stairs to the courtyard door. It was closed as usual, but not for long. Old Signora Boni came back from the market and opened it with her key. She was so busy pulling her wheeled shopping cart up the single step while not dropping her cane that she didn't notice Regina slink out of the doorway.

This was not the first time Regina had been in the courtyard of the palazzo. Before he started the fall school term, Giulio used to play with her among the pots with their miniature lemon trees and behind the sculpted border of fragrant rosemary. A high wall and a big wooden door guarded the garden from the Calle Borgolocco, the busy alley that thousands of tourists used to get to Campo Santa Maria Formosa, a vast square with a Renaissance church.

On the other end of the courtyard was a wide dank dim tunnel that led to the water. Decades ago, small boats were stored in the space, but they were gone, replaced by two large garbage bins. On Tuesdays the garbage barge came to collect the waste. The trash men tied up at the *bricola,* two thick wooden poles angled together and moored in the bottom of the canal at the end of the tunnel.

Regina had never entered the tunnel. It was too damp, dark and smelly. But when she rounded the last terracotta pot a mouse ran out from under the hedge and scampered beneath the second garbage bin. Without a thought, Regina went after it. She stuck her head under the odoriferous container just in time to see the rodent streak through the opening to the canal. Regina gave chase.

Skidding to a stop at the edge where the water lapped just a foot below, Regina couldn't see the mouse, but she could hear the scritch scratch of tiny feet. She peered around the corner. There was the mouse on a narrow ledge running just inches above the water.

Hating to lose, Regina considered the odds of balancing on the ledge. *Beneath my dignity,* she decided. *Anyway there will be liver waiting for me up...*"

The courtyard door banged opened as Bruno, the terrier, bounded out. In less than a second he had Regina's scent and raced towards her.

Without thought, Regina jumped for the ledge that the mouse had taken ... and missed.

Down, down, under the water. Regina sank fast and then bobbed to the surface, her legs churning. She could hear Bruno barking and Signor Morosini yelling.... But not about her. There was the sound of the giant wooden door slamming and then ... silence. Nobody scooped her out of the water. A small wave washed over her head. She surfaced near the *bricola,* snagging the ancient wood with the claws of her left paw and then her right. She tried to climb the mossy wood, but only succeeded in keeping her head above water.

Hanging on to the pole, she was considering her next move when she heard human jabbering. Not in Italian. She turned her head to see a gondola gliding toward her. The gobbledygook was coming from two Japanese tourists. She knew they were from Japan because she watched manga cartoons on the internet with her jester after he finished his homework.

The man and woman were pointing at her while leaning over the side of the gondola. The man was taking photos with his cell phone. The woman was almost screaming. The gondolier, in his striped shirt and straw hat, stood upright on the stern, trying to keep the gondola upright.

"Sit down," he yelled in Italian. His clients did not understand the words, but they must have understood the tone. They sat back on the plump fringed pillows on the high-backed passenger bench.

The gondolier poled the black boat closer to the wall of the palazzo. It rocked back and forth as he stepped down in front of his clients and reached under the seats. He pulled out a net with a long handle.

Regina froze as the gondolier scooped the net under her haunches. As he brought it up around her, she refused to let go of the wood. He tugged. She lost the grip of her left paw. He pulled harder and her right claws gave way. So did the gondola. It started floating down the canal. The Japanese man was filming the rescue.

The gondolier scrambled back to his perch still holding Regina in the net out over the water. He grabbed the pole out of the *forcola*, the metal clamp on the stern, and pushed the gondola further away from the wall.

"*Buongiorno, Signor Gatto,*" he said. "I'm Giorgio, your *salvatore*. It's not every day I get to save a drowning cat." He grinned for the camera. "We're going to be famous on YouTube, I'll bet. At least in Japan."

Regina stared back at him. Is he talking to me? *she wondered.* Is he calling me "signor"? Doesn't he recognize a queen when he sees one?

What Regina didn't realize was that soaking wet was not her best look. Her fur was matted and stuck out in all directions. Her usually regal head was tiny without its luxurious ruff. Her grand tail was a skinny rope that could have graced a large white rat.

"Sorry, I can't have you dripping on my silk cushions or my clients, said Gondolier Giorgio. "And I can't steer well and hold you, too. You are heavier than you look."

"Are you saying I'm fat?" hissed Regina, struggling against the net.

Giorgio didn't seem to hear her. "Hey, none of that. If you keep jerking around, you'll end up back in the canal."

As they rounded the bend in the canal, a wide walkway, a *fondamenta*, opened up to the right. On the left the steep walls of the palazzos were broken only by ornate windows.

"I'll put you off on the *Fondamenta Preti, Signor Gatto*," said Giorgio. "You should be able to find your way home. That is, if you fell in near where we found you."

And how am I supposed to do that? wondered Regina.

The Japanese couple clapped their hands and cheered as Giorgio dumped Regina on the cobblestoned passageway beside the canal.

"Arrivaderci, Signor Gatto," *Giorgio yelled.* "Buona fortuna.*"*

"Good luck? That's all you have to say?" grumbled Regina. "You snatch me from my palazzo and abandon me without even a dry towel?"

A woman clip-clopping along on three-inch heels almost stepped on Regina's tail, sending her scampering for safe haven. The scent of warm bread distracted her so she failed to notice the baker with a large broom sweeping the front doorstep of his shop until the broom made contact with her left hip.

"Get out of here, vermin," he yelled.

She zipped down the narrow alley behind the bakery and sought refuge in a large paper bag lying on its side. Paper bags had been favorites of hers in games of hide-and-seek with Giulio. This one smelled of the flour that Paola used to make pasta.

Time to make a plan, she thought. Within two minutes the exhausted Regina was fast asleep.

"Anchovy pizza or fried fish, Casanova?"

Regina woke to hear two of her kind discussing dinner right outside of her paper shelter. She peeped out, trying not to make a sound, but failed.

"Yikes!" yipped a high-pitched female voice. "Do you think it's a mouse?"

"No, much bigger than a snack," answered a tomcat. "Could be a whole meal. Let me take care of it for you, Fosca."

A large paw, claws extended, swiped through the mouth of the bag, just missing Regina's nose.

"Watch it, *Signor*," she hissed. "I'm no meal. Can't your nose tell the difference between a cat and a rat?"

A round black face with a white blaze down the nose and two topaz eyes appeared in the opening of the sack.

"Can't smell nothing but flour," said the cat. "You smell like a loaf of bread before it goes in the oven." He patted the bag over Regina's head. "Come out of there."

Regina emerged and shook herself.

"She looks like a loaf of bread, too," said Fosca, a dainty calico. "Doesn't she, Casanova?"

Regina picked and licked at her fur, but the flour and canal water had dried into clumps. She only succeeded in coating her tongue with dough and looking, if anything, more bedraggled.

"You aren't from this area," said the particolored cat. "We know all of the cats in the campos and calles around Santa Maria Formosa." She gave a delicate sniff of Regina's tail. "I'm Fosca and this handsome guy is Casanova."

The tomcat was twice Fosca's size. He seemed to have three white stockings, as if he had misplaced the one for his right front paw. His long midnight tail curved in an "S" over his back.

Regina gulped and focused on the smaller cat. "I don't think I am far from home," she responded to Fosca's observation. "I live in a palazzo on the canal back there." She pointed her nose in the direction that she thought she had come from. "My name is Regina."

"My, my, a *palazzo*." Fosca grinned at Casanova. "And Regina ... a royal name. Quite the fairy tale life."

"It was, until an evil dog chased me into the canal."

Casanova's ear twitched. "You let some mutt get the better of you? Palazzo living must make you soft."

Regina glared at him with narrowed eyes. "He caught me by surprise," she hissed.

"So why didn't you go home?" Fosca interjected.

"I'm not sure where my palazzo is. When I go outside these days, it's always in my roof-top garden."

"Wow," the sarcasm dripped from Casanova's tongue. "A private garden – *fancy*."

Casanova...," began Fosca, the referee.

"Private, except for my courtiers," added Regina.

Fosca stared, open-mouthed. "Your courtiers?"

"My lady-in-waiting, jester and footman."

"Oh, you mean the humans who feed you," said Casanova.

"Not just provide my meals. They also comb me, amuse me and are at my beck and call." Regina gave the two cats a defiant glare. "It took me months to train them with only the power of my mind. They are hopeless at learning our language."

"That's not so special," Fosca declared. "You don't need to be trapped inside to have all of that. Casanova and I have Signorina Foscanni and Signora Pratezzi who feed us." Her long pink tongue flicked out over her black and orange nose.

"And look at us compared to you," sniped the tomcat. "We're gorgeous and clean." He smoothed a paw up over his forehead and back behind his ears as if he was showing off his coiffure. "You can't take care of yourself and it shows. You're just a *pet*."

Regina huffed and picked at her clumpy tail. "Now look…"

Casanova kept going. "We see it all of the time. It's all of the 'kept' ones that look like a mess out here in real life. Ribs sticking out, ratty fur, drippy noses and eyes. The wild, free ones, like Fosca and me, are always groomed and fit."

"Speaking of being fed, weren't we trying to decide where to dine tonight?" Fosca turned to Regina. "Are you hungry? Want to join us or do you have to get back to you palazzo and royal court?"

Regina pushed away her anger. "I could eat. I missed my afternoon liver patê. Do you know where I can get some?"

"*La di da* … liver patê … let me think," Casanova scrunched his brow, scratched his chin and then swung his head to stare Regina down, invading her space. "No, your highness, liver patê is not on the menu tonight."

"You don't have to be sarcastic," said Regina. "I would go home if I knew… "

"Casanova, be nice." Fosca licked his ear. "You just aren't using your head. We can get crostini with chicken liver at Do Mori over across the Rialto Bridge. And we might find some fried fish balls and pickled sardines. The humans are finishing their afternoon *cicchetti*."

Regina's stomach rumbled, the thought of sardines made her mouth water. Maybe a day away from home wouldn't be so bad. She'd find the palazzo by tomorrow. Other things were on her mind now.

"Do you know where the nearest litter box is?"

Once the three cats left the tiny alley behind the bakery, the world became a chaotic mass of feet and legs, voices in all languages, smells of enticing sauces and grills mixed with putrid odors of discarded banana skins and orange peels, dropped cones of gelato with a hint of fish guts and spoiled chicken.

"How do you tolerate this," panted Regina, trying to follow as closely in the paw prints of her two new friends. *I've never had cat friends before.* The random thought almost made her miss Casanova's reply.

"It's the adrenaline rush we crave! Without all of this the world would be bland. And anyway, we sleep almost 18 hours a day. Without the aerobic workout, we start getting fat like you."

"Quit talking you two," said Fosca as she peered around a corner and planned their route through Campo San Lio. "Concentrate on not getting stepped on or tripping a human."

Five minutes later, Regina thought she was hallucinating that the street was climbing into the sky. They were crouched under a cart laden with jewel-toned masks and beribboned jesters' sticks. "Where are all of those humans going? They climb up there and then disappear."

"That's the Rialto Bridge. They're crossing the Grand Canal," said Fosca. "That's where we are going, too."

"What's the Grand Canal?"

Casanova stared at her. "Haven't you seen the Grand Canal before?"

"I assume it is like the waterway that runs along behind my palazzo," Regina answered. "I'm not stupid, so it must be just a bigger version."

"You have no idea. So pay attention. No gawking. We are going to have to streak up to the top and back down the other side." Casanova turned to Fosca. "I'm going first and you follow our royal guest.

Bite her on the rear if she stops." He turned to Regina. "This is the most dangerous part of our journey. The tourists have no sense and there are more of them packed on this bridge than any other place in Venice. They'll try to feed you, kick you, step on you, and even, pick you up…. Although maybe not you, since you look pretty disgusting. That's another reason to go fast – you're ruining our reputation."

"Harrumph," Regina harrumphed.

"Stay close behind Casanova, Regina. He's going to run along the balustrade."

"What's a balustrade?" asked Casanova.

"The railing, you ninny," Fosca yowled. "Get going."

They raced up the white stone bridge until they got to the top where Regina glanced to the left through the carved railing and came to an abrupt stop. Fosca leapt over her. "What the…?"

"Oh my, oh my, oh my," Regina was leaning off the side of the bridge. "Amazing! Why didn't I know this was here." Spread out in front of her was a huge expanse of water alive with vaporettos, gondolas and barges. The canal was lined with palaces of all colors embellished with Byzantine and Renaissance stonework, mosaics and glass.

"Regina, get moving. Casanova is already off the bridge."

"Gross! Mom, what's wrong with that cat?" Behind Regina and Fosca, a crew-cut blond boy was waving an iPhone on the end of a selfie stick at the two cats like a sword.

"Get away from there, Ralphie. It could be rabies." A woman dressed in culottes and flip-flops pulled the kid back by the neck of his t-shirt. "There are rats in this city."

Fosca seemed to double her normal size and her tail puffed out like a bottle brush. She hissed and spit at the boy and then swiped Regina's face with a open paw. "Snap out of it, Regina. I'm going to leave you here if you don't get moving. You are *not* going to get me caught."

The abject terror of being abandoned in the middle of a part of the world she never knew existed – before that moment – spurred Regina to follow Fosca as she sped down the Rialto and into the fruit and vegetable market, a sharp right turn at the end of the bridge.

Unable to catch her breath, Regina hoped the other two cats weren't going much farther. They sat under a stand of artichokes: both purple and green artichokes, huge artichokes on long stems, jars of tiny artichoke hearts drowning in olive oil, dried artichoke flowers and a huge bowl of artichoke bottoms, *fondi di carciofo,* floating in water.

"Exercise much?" Fosca softened the question with a grin. "It's usually Casanova huffing and puffing." She winked at him.

"Enough of that Fosca," he demurred. "This is boring. Let's show the lady of leisure what's left of the fish market. It's mostly closed for the day. But if she decides not to go back to the golden cage, she'll need to know where the best fish breakfast can be found."

The fruit and vegetable market was also shutting down. Big piles of waste, rotting tomatoes, limp cabbages, yellowing beans and empty produce boxes were being pushed onto the garbage barge. After passing the rows of tables they entered a covered *loggia*, a porch where the odors of fresh fish rose from a huge pile of discarded ice and the malodorous smell of rotting seafood coming from the giant garbage bins.

Fosca warned, "When we come here in the morning, it's like heaven on earth, but beware of the fish men who hate cats. Find the feline aficionados. There are a few. They will throw you a *branzino* head or a bit of calamari. There's a lady who will give you a chunk of tuna if you keep all of the other cats and the seagulls away from her stand. Those seagulls are mean."

"I know. I see them from my terrace," said Regina. "I remember once …"

Casanova interrupted, "All these aromas are making me hungry."

"Me, too." Fosca nodded.

"The fish market is not at its best right now," he observed. "Let's go on to Do Mori for dinner." He led the way off the *loggia*.

Fosca provided a running commentary as they slunk down the small back alleys. "Do Mori is a *bàcaro*, a tavern, which is so famous they named the *calle* after it. Myth has it that the famous Casanova, as opposed to our own friend, frequented this *bàcaro* three hundred years ago. It's the oldest of its type in Venice, dating back to 1462."

"I hope they have some *francobolli* with shrimp or cod," said Casanova.

"Postage stamps? *Francobolli* are for letters," Regina said, scrunching her nose in disdain.

"No, these are little sandwiches with yummy fillings," Fosca explained. "The name comes from the size."

"They are surely not going to serve them up to us on a platter," said Regina.

"Not to worry," Casanova yelled as he turned right on Calle dei Do Mori. "Roberto, the *barista*, is a friend of ours. He always plates up the discarded *cicchetti* for us and pours some water to wash it all down."

"I thought you said I was going to get liver *crostini*," whined Regina.

Fosca scuttled off, encouraging over her shoulder, "Wait and see."

And so it was. Beside the back door of the tavern the three cats ate like royalty on tiny pink shrimps, bits of octopus and squid, and *baccalà mantecato alla veneziana*, creamed salt cod, fluffy and white, served up on paper plates by Roberto.

Regina licked creamed chicken liver off the top of two crostini. *Ambrosia!* She could taste a bit of onion, olive oil and butter, and a dab of mustard. This was not the liver patê from a cat food can. *Why doesn't Paola make this for me?* Regina burped and swiped a licked paw over her whiskers.

"Slow down, princess," murmured Casanova. "You don't want to get sick." He pushed the last shrimp in Fosca's direction.

"Are you two a couple?" asked Regina, watching Fosca take a small bite and push the larger half back to him.

Fosca grinned. "No, just besties." She butted her head into her friend. "Casanova, despite his name, was shorn of his manhood by Dingo."

Regina didn't know how to respond. Why despite his name? How does one get shorn of his manhood? What or who was Dingo?

She started with the first question. "What does his name mean?"

Casanova puffed out his chest. "I'm one of a long line of lovers. Almost 300 years ago the first Casanova was a human who was world-famous for his amazing affairs with women. Every Italian tomcat has a bit of Casanova in him, or wishes he did. The original human, Giacomo Casanova, romanced royalty, knew popes and cardinals, and hung out with luminaries such as Voltaire, Goethe, and Mozart. I'm a modern-day lover in his style." The big black cat paced back and forth showing off his elegant physique.

Regina scratched her ear. "I don't know who those humans are. Would I know any felines who you romanced in the past?"

"Probably not, since you've been hiding away in your tower." He paused to think. "Perhaps you heard about the sweet pussy kept by that actress…"

Fosca interrupted, "All past history for our friend here. His days of seduction ended last year."

Regina watched the tomcat become very interested in grooming his tail. "Why? What happened?"

"His important bits were removed?"

"What do you mean?"

Fosca looked uncomfortable. "I guess you have all of your parts."

"Of course I do."

"Me, too, but many of our kind don't. Casanova got trapped last year and they clipped him before they brought him back to Campo Santa Maria Formosa. No more catting around for him. No more romance for him."

"That's not true," he protested. He took a swipe at her nose.

Fosca ducked and backed up, taunting, "No more kittens with his handsome face."

"That's true," he mumbled.

"I understand." Regina hid a grin behind a paw. "As a queen of the rare Turkish Angora breed, it is expected that I will pass along my qualities. I had a litter of kittens a year ago. One of my babies graced the cover of Paris Match when the French Prime Minister's wife sat for an interview. The three others live in Berlin, Rome and Florence. My lady-in-waiting told me last week that a new suitor had been found for me. I should be having Christmas kittens. ... That is if I ever *get* home."

Fosca ignored the last comment. "I've had four litters. That's why I'm hanging out with Casanova. I need a break. He's big enough that he scares off the others without having to get into big fights."

"Where are your children?

"I see them around. I used to be part of a clan in Parco della Regina in Castello. Some of my babies are still there. They're big now. And Dingo found my last litter so those are all doomed to be house cats forever."

"What's Dingo?"

"Before you get into that disagreeable subject, I think we should find a place to bed down for the night," said Casanova.

"How about Rocco's gondola at San Tomà?"

"Great, let's get moving."

Regina repeated her question. "But what's Dingo?"

"Dingo is the reason Casanova can't father kittens. Dingo is the reason my babies will never know the joy of being free felines in Venice." Fosca talked as she trailed Regina, who was following Casanova away from Do Mori and the best dinner she had ever had.

The sun had not set, but the *calles* were shadowed. The trio slunk along the side even though there were far fewer people in the area during the dinner hour.

Fosca continued, "It's an evil group of humans that have been around for fifty years. They claim it's in *defense* of what they call 'stray' cats, by which they mean free cats."

"They do feed a lot of our kind," said Casanova over his shoulder. "Every day they put out food in the major gardens and campos. They even built houses for free cats in the Castello gardens and near the San Lorenzo church."

Fosca nodded. "My kittens use two of the Dingo houses in Castello." She shot a sly look at Casanova's tail. "But what he won't tell you is that they also sterilize cats they catch and then adopt them out to be captive forever."

"Why is it called Dingo?"

"They used to capture abandoned dogs. Dingo was the name of the first stray dog they caught. But beware of thinking well of them. There are no free dogs in Venice anymore. That could happen to us."

"So they captured Casanova?"

"Yes, he wasn't paying attention, sleeping in the sun in front of the Hotel Danielli. The concierge called Dingo and they came and netted him."

"They only kept me for a week. After the operation, the Dingo people determined that I could never live in captivity – not adoptable, they said – so they dropped me off in Campo Santa Maria Formosa, far from the Danielli. That's where I found Fosca."

"But where did they take Casanova after they netted him?"

"Don't know," he grumbled. "Don't want to know."

"I found out when my children were taken," said Fosca with a hard look at the tomcat. "The old grand dame Flavia, she's almost twenty and sits in the window of the bookshop in Campo Santa Maria Formosa, told me that Dingo used to have a sanctuary on San Clemente, a beautiful island in the lagoon, but in 1999 a bunch of humans bought the island, evicted the cats and built a luxury hotel and spa." She spat at a purple-haired teenager who knelt to take a photo of the cats crossing in front of the main door of the San Polo Church.

She continued, "Now Dingo has a larger place on the Lido island, in a place called Malamocco. They say there are about 200 cats there, poor souls."

"Regina, be very careful," said Casanova. "For instance, if you see yummy food inside a cage. That's how they get you. The first time you go inside and dine, all will be fine. But the next time or the time after that, a door will fall. You're caught and off to Lido. If you don't search out food in the market or at friendly places like Do Mori, if you are lazy, they'll catch you."

Regina stopped, wide-eyed, wondering whether to believe him.

"Enough of this scaredy-cat talk, Casanova," said Fosca. "Let's show our new friend where royalty and a cat really did rub elbows."

"Do you mean…?"

Fosca did a little jig. "Yes. Ninì."

"What's a Ninì?" asked Regina.

"Come on. Let's go." Casanova guided them over a small bridge before continuing the story. "Ninì was a white tomcat who lived near here in the San Polo neighborhood between the Basilica dei San Frari and the state archives."

Regina picked up the pace so she could hear him. "What are 'archives'?"

"It's a place with books and documents where cats are truly appreciated because they keep the mice from eating and nesting in the paper."

"So Ninì was famous for being a mouser?"

"No, Ninì is famous for being a social cat," Fosca explained. "You could say he had his own social media rep."

"Social media?"

"Today they call it 'trending'."

"I know what trending means," she said, eyes gleaming. "My lady-in-waiting and jester are both on Facebook. I even have my own page. Giulio maintains it."

"Whatever," said Fosca. "In 1890, they just called it being famous."

"Famous for what?"

"For being charming, I guess. You could take a lesson from that."

"Ninì hung out at a café and the owner was good at getting the word out," Casanova took back the story. "Once Verdi met Ninì, the rest, as they say, was history."

Regina pulled to a stop, again. "The Verdi who wrote operas?"

"You know opera?" asked Casanova.

Fosca snipped, "Don't all cats?"

Seeing a tour group cross the bridge following a guide with a Carnival Cruise flag on the end of a stick, Regina urged her friends on as she said, "I know more about opera than most cats. My footman Domenico works at La Fenice."

"The Venice opera house? Have you been there?"

"No. Until today, I hadn't been outside my palazzo."

"Hey, this way," Fosca yelled from an alley to the right. When they caught up, she added, "Did you know that there is an opera called Fosca?"

Regina's voice took on a superior tone, "You mean Tosca by Puccini?"

"Not Tosca. I mean Fosca, like me."

"I'm kidding you." Regina conceded. "Of course I know Fosca. The libretto was by Antonio Ghislanzoni, wasn't it? Didn't Fosca die in the end?"

"She took poison."

"Gruesome, " said Casanova. "But very romantic."

"Slow down," begged Regina. "Fosca, what about Ninì and Verdi? Did they get along?"

" I guess Ninì had a guest book...."

"Like my Facebook page."

"Did Verdi 'like' your Facebook page?" Fosca teased.

"No, but I do have 2,000 followers."

"Anyway," Casanova said, "like you Ninì had many fans, but his included a pope, a Russian Czar, and the Emperor of Ethiopia. They all wrote in Ninì's book."

"That's not a fair comparison. There are no Ethiopian Emperors or Russian Czars left in the world. I am followed by Taylor Swift, Russell Brand, Cameron Diaz, and George Clooney. They are modern royalty."

They entered the square in front of the Frari church.

"Wait ... there's more." Casanova and Fosca grinned at each other. "Ninì was visited by an actual and queen," they said in unison.

"What?"

"King Umberto I and Queen Margherita came to visit Ninì and signed her book. There's proof. I think the book still exists. Ninì, of course is long gone."

"Here we are," said Fosca. "This is Ninì's home, the Caffé dei Frari."

The café was closed. No humans were in sight. Regina looked up at a cat drawn on the maroon awning and the posted menu with an illustration of a cat about to munch on a mouse speared on a fork.

"Look over here on the façade," called Fosca. "There's a fresco of Ninì."

Regina gazed at the painting of a fluffy white cat with yellow eyes protecting, claws out, an ornate cup of coffee that rested on a book. Except for the eyes, he could have been a Turkish Angora, she thought.

"Cat lovers from all over the world still come here to see where Ninì lived," said Casanova. "Someday I am going to be as famous as Ninì.

"Maybe Do Mori will put your photo on its wall, Casanova." Regina tried to look completely serious, but inside she was laughing.

"Maybe," said Casanova. "I would prefer to be immortalized at Caffé Florian in Piazza San Marco. A more international exposure."

"I wonder if Giulio has put a notice on my Facebook page to let my followers know that I'm missing?"

The other two crowded closer. Fosca spoke first, "It's only been a few hours since you went into the canal. He may not have noticed you are gone."

"No, not possible. I help him do his homework every evening before he eats dinner. He'll know that I'm not in the apartment."

"Apartment?" Casanova sat bolt upright. "I thought you said you lived in a palazzo."

"Details, details. An apartment in a palazzo. What's the difference?"

Casanova shook his head and walked away. "Time to head off to San Tomà."

In response to Regina's questioning look, Fosca said, "Our friend Rocco usually ties up his gondola at the San Tomà traghetto stop each evening."

"There's nothing like a rocking gondola to assure a good night's sleep. It's down…"

"There's no way I'm going to get into another gondola." Regina sat down.

"… this alley." Casanova kept walking.

Fosca nosed Regina, urging her on. Tied up to the short wharf at San Tomà were two gondolas, covered in canvas.

"Rocco's is the one with the red cover." The end was loosely tied with a skinny rope through a metal ring. Fosca slipped under the canvas. "Come on, Regina."

Regina wasn't sure she wanted to cross the space over the water between the wharf and the bobbing gondola. Casanova acted the gentleman by standing on the gondola and stretching to the wharf. The boat stopped moving until Regina leapt across the small space.

Casanova and Fosca curled up and fell immediately asleep on one end of the upholstered high-backed bench. Regina thought of taking one of the two small chairs, topped by fat pillows, but decided to take the other end of the bench. She woke later when the bells of San Marco rang the midnight hour to find herself curled against the other two.

She mused, What is this new day going to bring?

Sunbeams slid down the canal early the next morning as the three cats padded over the Accademia Bridge.

"Let's see if we can catch a baby pigeon in Piazza San Marco or, even better, get a piece of brioche from a tourist at Caffè Florian," said Fosca. Regina, you are going to have to stay out of sight. If anything, you look worse this morning than yesterday. Horrible bedhead, like, all over. We have to find somewhere for you to bathe today."

"Yeah, we have a rep to maintain," said Casanova. "But don't worry, we'll bring you some breakfast. In fact, you two wait here. I'll check out the possibilities."

They rounded the corner and entered the *loggia* that bordered the square in front of the Basilica of San Marco. The porch was wet following a thorough cleaning. A water truck at the far end finished washing the empty piazza. Only a few pigeons moved across the space.

"We are a long way from my home," said Regina. "I can see the dome and the tower from my terrace, but they seem tiny. Here they look so big."

"I bet you didn't know that this was the spot of a famous cat tragedy." Fosca gazed at the top of the tower.

"What happened?"

"Back in 1902, the custodian of the tower kept a cat to clear the place of mice and rats. The tower was weak and the humans had lots of notice that it would fall. On the day it fell, they had cleared the entire piazza and the church of humans. But did they tell the poor cat? No, of course not! The tower fell and the cat was the only victim."

"That's horrible!"

Fosca declared, "This a warning to all housecats. Never let the humans take your freedom. It will always end in tragedy."

"Did she tell you that the caretaker's tabby cat was named Mélampyge?" the tomcat said, returning from the café. He dropped a piece of an eggy tart with pancetta on the ground in front of Regina. "And the best part of the story is that Mélampyge was also the name of famous lover Casanova's dog. Supposedly, he was a fox-terrier."

"Bruno, the monster who chased me into the canal was a terrier."

"That wasn't the important part of what I just told you," he grumbled.

Regina bit a corner off the tart and munched, throwing him a skeptical look. "How would they know what Casanova called his dog? I thought you said he lived 300 years ago."

"He wrote everything down. And the name was from classical Greek. It had something to do with Hercules." He spaced out for a moment and then focused again. "Anyway, the most important thing is the name is only given to those with black bottoms, or black tails, or ... you get the idea." He turned to the calico. "Come on, Fosca. There is a cat lady from England at Florian. She'll probably ask the waiter for milk."

He watched Regina swallow the last piece of the tart. "Sorry, Regina, but the waiters know us. They'll chase you away.

"Go in that alley and wait for us," said Fosca.

Regina slunk away. She watched the two cats approach a plump woman seated at a small table outside of a café. She wondered why she could smell liver from the café so far away. *I must be imaging the aroma. Humans don't eat liver for breakfast*, she thought.

She looked down the alley. There must be a restaurant, *she thought.* I know liver when I smell it. I bet there are those crostini things around here.

She walked into the dim end of the alley. There was a restaurant kitchen door and a paper bowl of liver paté. She did not notice the cage until the door dropped behind her as she munched. *Trapped!*

Casanova and Fosca heard her cries and came running.

"Sorry, old girl," said Casanova. "We warned you. Nothing we can do. Dingo has you. Don't worry, they're nice, sort of."

A key clicked in the lock of the door near the cage. Casanova and Fosca scurried away. The door opened. A man leaned out. "You are right," he said to someone inside the kitchen. "Caught an ugly one."

Who are you calling ugly? Regina backed into the corner of the cage, hissing.

"Call the number they gave us." He went back inside.

The two free cats came back. "We can't stay," said Fosca. "When they let you go, come to Campo Santa Maria Formosa and ask for us."

Casanova nodded. "*Buona fortuna*, your highness." He ducked out of the alley. Fosca followed.

Two hours later, a man walked down the alley. Regina hissed and backed into a corner away from the door. Her ruff, albeit still clumped with flour, doubled in size.

He ignored her, threw a cloth over the cage, picked it up and carried it to a boat. A motor fired up and they bumped off over the low swells.

Humiliating ... totally humiliating ... don't they recognize quality when they see it? Regina thought that Dingo could inhabit a unique circle of hell. Instead of burning coals or constant wailing, this hell brimmed with baths, injections, medicated paste, and dry crunchy tasteless kibble. A world without liver pâté. Peopled with Tomaso, Portia, Stefania and Emily, all of whom were unceasingly cheerful.

The worst part was the comb-out. Tomaso held her down as Emily pulled the tangles out of her wet fur first with a rubber curry brush and next with a narrow-toothed steel comb. As miserable as she was, she felt relieved that she wasn't the long-haired tomcat across the room who was being shaved by Portia and Stefania. Regina only lost one matted clump of fur on her stomach that couldn't be combed out. After a quick snip with scissors, Regina was allowed to take a nap.

After two days in solitary confinement, Regina was released into an enclosure of female cats and kittens of both sexes. She immediately determined who was the chattiest inmate, a silver-gray Persian mix named Pamela.

From Pamela she learned that the enclave included four areas: one each for males and females, a series of cages for the antisocial or dangerous, and the hospital wing.

"Why are there no tomcats in here?"

"They don't let us mix until we are what they call 'fixed.' You can tell the unsexed ones by the clipped left ear."

"They are going to cut off my ear?"

"No, just nip off a little piece. If you have a clipped ear they won't bring you back from Dingo, if you can behave in public."

"When will this horrible thing happen to us?"

"The surgeon comes in three day's time. But you clearly are what they consider a pet. They may wait until they try to find your humans."

"How will they find Paola and Domenico?" Regina hoped the staff figured it out soon. She wasn't sure how long she would be able to tolerate the communal litter box in the enclosure.

"Usually humans contact Dingo when one of us go missing. My human won't call because she is dead. They found me under her bed. I hadn't eaten in days."

"So what is going to happen to you?"

"Since I'm not feral and can't survive on my own, they will keep me here until someone wants to give me a forever home. My lady made sure I couldn't have children years ago so I get to keep my ear intact.

I've become the nanny here when litters are brought in. I am also the official hostess of this yard."

"I hope to be going back to my palazzo before my ear is clipped, so to speak."

Later that day, Stefania came into the yard with three kittens, who appeared to be about two-months-old. "Pamela, will you take care of these three?" She put the kittens in the corner.

Regina thought there was something familiar about them. There was a calico girl, an orange male and a white girl with an orange tail. "Pamela, do you know where these kittens are from?"

"I heard a rumor that they were in a nest behind a fish place called Osteria alle Testiere in Calle Mondo Novo. Their mother was away hunting when they were found."

"I bet these are Fosca's babies."

"They probably won't remember her. I think they were only a week old when they were found. They will become housecats. Humans always want to adopt kittens."

Regina went over to the siblings. "I think I know your mother." She spent the next hour regaling the youngsters with tales of Fosca and Casanova. "I'm sorry I know nothing of your father, but Casanova would make a wonderful godfather or uncle." They had all curled up, fast asleep by the time she finished her story. She sat watching over them, wondering for the first time how her own children were and where they lived now.

In the next three days, Regina started each morning wondering if her courtiers would take up the crusade to come rescue her, but then as Fosca's kittens came to hear more stories, she enjoyed being the center of attention. Regina sat on a raised pedestal wrapped in sisal rope, a couple of feet above her audience, made up of not only the three young cats, but also a number of the other residents, telling them the tales of Ninì and Mélampyge, as well as stories about her life in the palazzo. Pamela snoozed on her own box in the shade across the enclosure.

Either Portia or Stefania groomed the two long-haired cats each day, talking about princesses and a queen ruling the lagoon. Regina and Pamela assumed that the conversation was about them. They argued about who was the princess and who was the queen. They couldn't figure out who was another princess. Nobody else in the yard qualified according to them.

Four days later, there was a commotion outside the enclosure. Portia opened the gate and a beautiful girl with long golden curls rushed in, talking a mile a minute.

"This is, like, so *cool*, Portia. Last year the charity for the queen's *burchiello* was the children's hospital so each member of the royal court had a cute kid sitting beside them." She waved a languid hand at the Dingo residents. "This year my barge is just going to have my princesses and a bunch of cats in honor of

Dingo. People will like the pussy cats, but they will be looking at me."

Regina and Pamela exchanged a baffled look. Who was this noisy girl? And what did it have to do with them?

"Gloriana, we are so pleased that the work of Dingo is going to get some attention," Portia said. "Having our cats on the royal *burchiello storico* in the Historical Regatta as well as a banner asking everyone to help our cause is so important to us. But we need to carefully consider which cats are on the barge. It is a boat in the middle of the Grand Canal after all."

Gloriana nodded, her sunshine hair sweeping back and forth over her bare shoulders. One of the kittens sitting beside Regina looked as if he was going to jump to catch a swinging curl. She put a fluffy white paw on his orange head.

"I understand," said Gloriana, queen of the *Regata Storica*. "Of course we can't have any feral cats sitting with us. They might scratch or bite. We might catch something."

Portia frowned. "What I meant was that stray cats who have never had a home would be frightened to be on a boat. They are scared of human contact."

"Right. That's what I said." Gloriana scanned the yard. "What about that gorgeous white one and maybe the Persian pussy over there?"

"What's she saying?" Pamela hissed at Regina, who shrugged a shoulder.

Portia nodded. "Both of those cats came from home environments. If you and your princesses spend some time with these two and the others we choose. We are also going to have them outfitted with collars and some sort of leash so the cats are secure on the barge."

"*Cool!* We can color-coordinate the colors with our historical costumes. Mine is emerald green. I want the white cat on my lap." She swooped toward Regina who backed up so fast that both she and the kitten fell off her pedestal.

Portia stepped in front of the girl, holding up a restraining palm. "Slowly, slowly, Gloriana. You have to move bit by bit when approaching a cat who doesn't know you."

"Okay, I guess." Gloriana moved toward Regina again. "What's her name?"

"We don't know. We call her Valide because she is a Turkish Angora and that's the title of the Sultan's wife."

"She's a Turkish queen then. And I'm the queen of the *Regata Storica*. We're perfect for each other."

"The Persian cat is Pamela. We know where she came from so we know her given name." Portia opened the gate and called out, "Stefania, can you bring a couple of chairs. Gloriana wants to make friends with our queen bees."

Queen bees? Regina frowned. *Is she talking about Pamela and me. We aren't insects. I am a queen, but Pamela would be more like a duchess, I think.* She scurried out of reach over to the silvery Persian, jumping onto Pamela's box. "Do you know what is going on?"

"If I understand correctly, Regina" she answered, "we are about to be 'honored' with a ride down the Grand Canal…"

"*Fabulous!* I saw the Grand Canal four or five days ago," Regina interjected.

"…on a historic barge, called a *burchiello.*"

"On the water? In a boat?" *Regina caterwauled.*

"What's wrong with Valide?" asked Gloriana as she took a seat, placing her Hermes purse on the ground beside her.

"She may be a little nervous around strangers," said Stefania as she offered the second chair to her colleague. "Let me see if I can hand her to Portia first and then you can try to hold her." She slowly walked to where the two cats sat and kneeled to scratch both of them under their chins at the same time. "Ladies, we have a guest. Let's be friendly."

"I hope the kittens chew on her purse," Regina said to Pamela.

This is truly the way my life was supposed to be, thought Regina, cushioned on an elaborate azure silk pillow fringed in gold. Her neck was bejeweled with a crystal-studded collar from which ran a long narrow ribbon that Gloriana was supposed to hold. But the queen of the *Regata Storica* took her responsibility to her adoring subjects much too seriously to pay much attention to the elegant white cat on her lap. She waved to the crowds on one side of the Grand Canal and then to the masses on the other side.

As the royal barge passed under the Rialto Bridge, Regina remembered back to the evening of her last best meal. She may be a regal cat but a steady diet of Dingo's kibble was getting boring. She gazed down from their perch on a throne placed behind the court of royal princesses. Pamela gave her a wink from the lap of a plump maiden resplendent in rose silk. Each of the other five girls held a cat from Dingo: two older neutered toms and three females, who had formerly been housecats. No kittens or feral cats had been selected for the festival ride.

In front of the *burchiello* was the state barge of the Venetian doges, the *bucintoro,* on which most of the rich and noble men of the city rode, dressed in historical costumes.

Regina overheard Portia telling Stefania the day before that this was the first time the replica of the *bucintoro* was going to be used in a festival. She said that the last of the original barges for the Venetian head of state had been destroyed in 1798 when Napoleon ordered it destroyed, less for the sake of its golden decorations than as a political gesture to symbolize his victory over the Veneto. French soldiers broke up the carved wooden and gold decorations of the ship into small pieces, carted them to the island of San Giorgio Maggiore and set fire to them to recover the gold. "The ship burned for three days," Portia reported, "and French soldiers used 400 mules to carry away its gold." Regina wondered what a mule was, but Pamela didn't know, either.

Regina took in a long breath. The salty breeze mixed with Gloriana's tuber rose scent. Just then the festival queen ran her long fingers all the way down Regina's back, causing a reflexive arch and much waving of her plumy tail. Regina took the opportunity to resettle herself on the pillow as Gloriana went back to the business of waving. Now Regina was facing the left side of the canal. The water churned with hundreds of gondolas and longer boats with a dozen or more rowers, all in jewel-toned costumes. Flags flew from the boats and barges. Large multicolored silk banners hung from the palazzos and bridges along the canal.

"*Regina!* Regina, look up here!" She heard her name being called by her kind through the human noise. It wasn't Pamela because she was down, not up. Their barge was about to go under the Accademia Bridge. She gazed toward the sky and caught a glimpse of a small particolored face next to the large black visage dominated by a white blaze. *It couldn't be*, she thought. But then she was staring at the underside of the bridge with its crisscrossing metal bars and huge water pipes.

She scrambled on the pillow, bracing her front paws on Gloriana's shoulder, waiting for them to emerge on the other side.

"Velide, *stop that*," the queen yelled. Regina ignored her. They were almost out of the bridge's shadow. Her pupils narrowed as she focused on the openings in the wooden balustrade.

There they are! It's Fosca and Casanova! She called to the two cats, who had squeezed through the legs of the tourists standing at the railings. They stretched their necks to peer down at the barge. She could see them clearly now.

"Not a bad gig if you can get it, Regina," yelled Casanova. "You really are a queen now."

"We were worried about you," called Fosca.

Regina started with the most important part. "Fosca, I met your children. They're beautiful. I told them all about you."

Fosca was speechless, but her expression told of her relief and happiness.

"Come and find us when you get out of prison." Casanova patted the side of the bridge with a paw.

Regina was now too far away to hear.

"Get off me, you *fiend!*" Gloriana had two hands gripped around her middle in a most uncomfortable way. Regina dug her claws in to the emerald silk sleeve. The tug-of-war commenced.

"*Regina!*" This time the voice was human. Both queens paused in their battle and looked over the right side of the *burchiello*.

A few feet below their throne and almost even with the gilded railing of the barge was Giulio, Regina's jester. He sat on a high seat in the back of a dragon boat with a large drum in front of him. Because he stopped drumming when he saw his lost cat, the twelve paddlers lost their rhythm and the boat slowed. The barge moved past.

Giulio started drumming again, yelling to the crew, "That's my cat on top of the queen. I have to get to her. *Paddle!*"

The dragon boat pulled even again. With an abrupt jerk, Regina pulled free of Gloriana's sleeve, leaving only a small rip, and jumped to the railing. Without another thought she leaped into the middle of the drum. Giulio wrapped his arms around her amidst the cheers of his crewmates and the screams of the festival queen, whose crown had been knocked askew.

Giulio wrapped Regina's ribbon leash around his hand, leaving enough length so he could settle her between his feet below the drum. "Let's get to the end of this parade in double-time," he said, picking up the drumsticks.

Regina didn't even mind the noise. She had found Giulio! She was going home!

At Piazza San Marco, Giulio's school boat docked to be met by all of the parents, including Paola and Domenico. Regina enjoyed the shocked looks on their faces when their son hoisted her over his head, perhaps from the shock of seeing her or maybe because Giulio almost overbalanced into the water.

They took turns carrying the white cat with her new fancy collar as they walked home. The chatter of their voices was the soundtrack of Regina's happiness.

But that's not the end of the story. Two weeks later, Regina was lazing on her roof-top dais when on the terracotta rooftop of the abandoned palazzo across the alley she saw Fosca and Casanova creeping around a cracked chimney pot.

"My goodness gracious," she exclaimed. "How did you find me?"

"You're famous," Fosca said. "Your address was in the newspaper story about the ruckus at the *Regata Storica*. Signora Pratezzi read it to us before she left our dinner on the paper."

Casanova licked a paw and cleaned a cobweb off his ear. "It took us awhile to figure out how to get up to this roof. We've been up here twice and decided that had to be your terrace, but you were never there."

"Can you two figure out how to get up on this building?"

"Casanova is working on that." Fosca scratched her side with a back foot."

"Maybe we can go on adventures together. It's very dull here now that I know about the rest of the world."

Casanova scanned the roof-top garden. "But you wouldn't want to give all of this up, right?"

"No, but I miss you and Fosca."

Fosca wrinkled her nose and winked at the big black cat beside her. "He'll figure it out. We'll all be off on adventures soon."

Just then Paola emerged from the stairs carrying a tall Caldera cactus in a glazed pot. "Regina, it's about time for your liver paté."

Regina raised a paw to her friends, rose, stretched and made her way along the top of the railing. Casanova and and Fosca watched her go before focusing on a couple of seagulls wheeling across the sky to the San Marco bell tower.

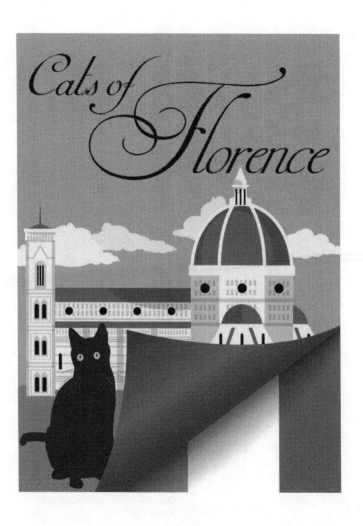

CATS OF FLORENCE:

Dante, Guido & Gattone

Could I have done something to avert what now has become widely known as *A Terrifying Tale: Trapped in the Tower*? I contemplated this as I scratched my ear with the claws of my left hind paw. It wasn't my fault. As usual, I came up with a brilliant plan and my brother Dante did something stupid (like bite a kid on his ankle), and everything went to hell. Or I should say *inferno*, since we were in Florence and it was Dante who got us imprisoned in the tower. But let's not get ahead of ourselves. I'll tell the tale this way:

It was a dark and stormy night when things went from bad to down right catastrophic.

I've always wanted to start one of my stories with the words "it was a dark and stormy night" but this was the only time it was actually *dark* and *stormy*. Dante, who will transcribe my dictation of this tale, told me that Elmore Leonard (master of the hard-boiled plot) said never to start a story with weather. But I never listened to Dante and, unlike him, I don't read. So even though I loved watching *Get Shorty* and *Jackie Brown* on Kate's iPad, I've never read Mr. Leonard's books.

It was a dark and stormy night. We were high above the stone streets of Florence inside an abandoned medieval tower in the historic center of the city I commonly deride as Renaissance Disneyland. This is not Florence, Florida or Florence, Colorado or Florence, South Carolina. What would a medieval tower be doing in any one of those places?

So as I was saying, it was a dark and stormy night outside the thousand-year-old tower where Dante and I were trying to convince our friend Gattone that it was better to brave the elements, rather than face the wrath of Kate and Giovanna.

To tell the absolute truth, which I almost always do (except when the feelings of others are involved or to get myself out of a jam), the tower wasn't completely abandoned. The bottom three floors housed a musty, dusty museum to honor all things Garibaldi. Who was Garibaldi? He was one of the most honored/despised leaders of Italy's unification movement of the late 1800s. He was such a great military tactician that Abe Lincoln asked him to assume command of the Northern troops. Garibaldi declined. He probably knew he would never find a good plate of pasta south of New Jersey. Final fact: Garibaldi has a British biscuit named after him. But I learned all of these details later while trying to flesh out this tale.

Dante, Gattone and I were crouched on the stairs of the abandoned portion of the Torre della Castagna, debating our next move as the thunder rolled and the lightning flashed and the rain blew sideways past the small square holes in the tower walls.

For those who know nothing about medieval Italian architecture, Florence in the 14th century (before the Black Death swept through the city in 1348 and they learned that the rat-eating cat was man's best friend) was a city of about 100,000 humans. A fortified wall surrounded it. Inside the wall nobody got along with anybody else outside their own family and sometimes not even then. (Dante wanted to insert a reference to the Capulets and the Montagues, but they were in Verona, not Florence.) The rich people built towers to live in for protection from their next-door neighbors. At one time, there were over three hundred towers in Florence, of which the Torre della Castagna was one. Towers did not have windows because the hostile neighbors might decide to shoot burning arrows through any hole bigger than a human hand-width. Towers had a lot of small square holes that let in light and air (and the sound of rain and thunder).

There I crouched, looking out of one of those measly little holes (too small for Gattone to squeeze through), thinking about how we ended up in this predicament and trying to decide what to do next.

Our stuck-in-a-tower-during-a-storm plight started simply enough that afternoon. It was a Thursday at about four thirty.

The three of us lived about three streets closer to the Duomo from the Torre della Castagna. The Duomo is the cathedral with the big dome. (Duomo means "cathedral" in Italian and has nothing to do with the dome, even though the Duomo in Florence has the third biggest dome in the world.)

Gattone was a fat cat (Italians would know this from his name) and never got out of the house. He lived in the apartment below ours.

Kate, Dante and I shared one of the two apartments on the top floor of a building constructed in the 13th century. None of the housing in the historic center, be it a palazzo or a home for regular folks, was very tall, but the building we lived in was only three stories. On the street level there was a gelateria. The next floor up was where Gattone, Giovanna and her husband, Roberto, lived in a huge apartment, which was only right because they owned the whole building. Above them, up two flights of stairs was a landing with two doors, which opened to our home and a slightly bigger apartment rented by Francesca, a philosopher, writer, cook-extraordinaire, and clarinet player. She was born in Florence.

Kate was an American from San Francisco. Known for living with two intelligent cats, Dante and me, she also spent time touring around Florence with clients who wanted to "go where the tourists don't go" (virtually impossible) and blogging about her experiences as a single-woman-of-a-certain-age living in Italy. She frequently wrote about Dante and me without our consent.

On that Thursday, Gattone lolled in his garden with the sun warming his golden brown, black-striped fur. I was in my usual afternoon spot on the windowsill overlooking his garden. I was not allowed to go out the back door of our apartment, which leads to a balcony that is only a short hop down to Gattone's spacious garden, because allegedly I picked fights with him. Even though I was much smaller, Giovanna claimed that, at least once, he was "traumatized" by me.

"Guido, I'm bored," said my alleged former victim, looking up at me from his perch on the broken garden bench that Giovanna had been trying to get Roberto to fix for months.

Thoroughly grooming my left paw, I ignored him for a minute or three to make him suffer. "If you hadn't been such a tattletale, I could be down there right now helping you catch that lizard climbing the wall behind your ears," I said, emphasizing my disinterest in his ennui with a wide yawn.

Gattone's head whipped around and he leapt, missing the lizard by at least ten inches. When he landed, the rotting board gave way with a screech, as I knew it would, dumping him in a small puddle. Giovanna had recently watered the plants on the terra cotta terrace.

"Gattone, *che è successo?*" We both could hear Giovanna ask what had happened from her usual spot in the kitchen, but she didn't leave the pot of *ribolita* I could smell cooking on her stove.

Licking the big damp spot on his left hip, Gattone sulked in silence.

"Hey, *amico*, I didn't mean for that to happen," I lied.

Gattone glared up at me on the sill behind the wire mesh screen. He stretched up his left leg up behind his neck. It was not a good look for him, although I was impressed that he could maintain the position.

"I was not a tattletale." Gattone referred to my earlier accusation. "You left a scratch on my cheek and bite marks on my rump. Giovanna threatened to take me to the vet if they got infected. She had only you or Dante to blame and he's always a *gatto gentile*. And anyway, he spends most of his time in Francesca's place sleeping on one ancient book or another."

"Okay, okay, point taken," I said, yawning again to show it wasn't important. "It's just that Kate, the all powerful, sentenced me to the life of a house cat. She thinks I will never venture forth again."

"That's just cruel." He cocked his head in thought. "But that's what I am. A house and garden cat. Just life in the apartment – of course, it *is* twice as big as yours – and the garden. You're going to become as bored and fat as I am."

"Bored and stupid. You aren't listening to me. I said that Kate *thinks* I'm a house cat. I sure haven't let her in on the fact that I can get out through the bathroom window."

"But that's impossible. Kate's bathroom is tiny and the window is high."

"Hey, I'm only two years old. I haven't packed the weight on like you, old eunuch. Once I've batted down the toilet lid, I'm a third of the way there. All it takes is an open window and good aim."

"I'm impressed. Then it is just a hop down to Francesca's terrace. But after that, where can you go?"

I had Gattone firmly hooked. Now all I had to do was reel him in, like a big catfish. "Want to see?"

"How can I? I'm stuck here in this garden."

"Can you climb the trellis in that corner that covers the wall up to Francesca's porch?"

"Maybe," Gattone said, eyeing the thick foliage of the jasmine vines covering the iron trellis.

"Try it. If you make it, I'll join you. The bathroom window is open and Kate is out on a date with that idiot Stefano."

"I'm not sure . . ."

I interrupted, "You're bored. You want adventure. I'm offering. You choose."

"All right, but Dante has to come, too. I'm not going with just you. Remember last time? I still have a scab on my butt."

"No problem. After you make it to Francesca's terrace, I'll go get him."

It was not a thing of beauty, but Gattone clawed and pushed and scrambled up the vines. Blooms and sprigs of greenery flew off. Jasmine and cat sweat perfumed the air. Surprisingly he didn't make much noise and Giovanna didn't notice.

I went to look for Dante. As usual, he was asleep. Our kind, on average, sleep about eighteen hours in every twenty-four. Dante seemingly laid claim to two of my hours and as his brother, I am happy to oblige. Also, as usual, he slept on an open book. This time it was an English translation of Michelangelo's love poems that Kate had borrowed from Francesca. Kate was blogging about the sculptor's love life. *Boring.*

Usually I wake Dante up by licking his ears. He hates that.

"Dante!" I made it sound like someone had set fire to the house and I pounced on him for good measure. "We have to help Gattone!"

"What? What?" Dante had completely lost that call-of-the-wild skill of sleep to wakefulness in a split second. He even removed himself from the book so his first shoulder to hip stretch didn't rip or crumple the pages. "Why did you jump on me?"

"Didn't you hear? Gattone is trapped on Francesca's terrace. He needs our help." I raced toward the bathroom, knowing that in his befuddled state, Dante would follow. Book smarts, he had. Common sense, not so much.

It worked like all of my plans do. I hopped on the toilet seat (lid down), leapt to the windowsill (window open, no screen), and down onto Francesca's small iron terrace table. Dante followed as if by instinct, but then his brain caught up to his body when his paws hit the sill.

"What the flying fur ball?" Dante yelled trying to cling to the ledge. His tail was up, providing ballast. However, even though he was my littermate, Dante was quite a bit larger than I. Most of his extra weight was in his rear quarters. If I was being catty, I'd say he was a fat-assed cat, something that sadly happens to felines who have been emasculated. (I, too, was de-balled, but I kept my fighting trim.)

"Come on down," I said in my best imitation of a talk show host. Being allegedly confined to quarters, I watched too much television.

Dante overbalanced into the terrace, missing the table and landing four-footed on the terra cotta floor. "Gattone, are you all right?" He gave our neighbor the

international feline salute, nose to anus, and then the
Italian two cheek greeting.

"All right? I'm more than all right. I just climbed
that wall and Guido has promised me an adventure.
Let's go." Gattone leapt like a kitten to join me on the
table.

Dante glared green-eyed up at me. "You sly puss.
What danger? Why am I here?" His tail was
horizontal, flipping back and forth. Not a good sign.

I was saved by the *gatto grande*. "I insisted that you
come along," said Gattone. "I can't really trust Guido
after that last episode, if you know what I mean?"

"I recalled the time he almost disemboweled you.
Is that what you are referencing?" Dante hissed. "You
are seriously thinking about taking off on an
adventure with a cat with anger management issues,
my friend?"

I plopped down beside my brother, rolled to
expose my very cute tummy, and purred a second
before trying to mute his sarcasm with flattery. "Hey,
bro, no need to get personal. Gattone and I are
mending fences with a little team building exercise.
Three makes a better team than two, and you know
how we enjoy your company." The last bit was a lie.

Gattone weighed in. "Dante, I am dying of
boredom. The house is comfy, the garden is great, but
nothing happens. Roberto's always gone. Giovanna is
only interested in her plants. I've lost my purpose as a
cute diversion. I think I'm having a mid-life crisis.
Wait until you get to be my age. The last excitement I
had was two years ago when that baby pigeon fell

from its nest on the roof into the garden. Fighting off the mother was fun, but the kid was just a two-bite snack."

Dante sat and contemplated his paw before giving it a lick. He looked at me, still on my back. I got tired of the submissive role, so I rolled to my feet and went off to check out the bee buzzing around the pot of roses in the corner. Dante turned to look at his friend.

Unlike me, Kate regularly let my brother out on to our balcony so he could visit the lower garden. Many a time I had to watch from the window as the two pals groomed each other in the sun among the flowers. To make things worse, from there Dante got to go through the cat hatch into Gattone's home, a welcome guest. Just the thought of it made me want to call off the whole adventure plan.

"Gattone," said Dante, "you are not so young or fit, anymore. These midnight rambles Guido takes, if I can hazard a guess, include rooftops, stairs, tunnels, and, at times, require bursts of speed."

"But I just told you. I climbed the jasmine vines. I made it up here with no problem. Tell him, Guido." Gattone was getting a little whiny.

We all turned to look six feet down the ragged jasmine vine to the garden floor.

"I promised him an adventure," I purred, brushing up against Dante's ear, giving it a little lick as I passed.

"You've had your adventure, just in that climb," said Dante. "I'm getting Francesca. She'll take you down the inside stairs to your apartment." He turned to scratch on the long shutters covering the door that led to Francesca's kitchen.

"When the shutters are closed, she's not there," I said.

"Moldering mice," Dante spat. My brother thought that swearing was for cretins, so he came up with these strange exclamations. It drove me crazy. What was wrong with good old cuss words? "Francesca told me," he continued, "that she was going to a seminar in Siena on Pliny the Elder. She doesn't get back until tomorrow."

Not only did Dante, the perfect pussy, get access to the apartment downstairs, but he also got to visit Francesca whenever he wanted. It seemed he preferred to spend more time with that smart Italian girl than with Kate, our companion and savior. Francesca had a library with books in four languages. We both can understand spoken English and Italian, although we never let the humans know this. Dante went a step further and taught himself to read in both of those languages, plus Spanish and Russian, just by pawing through (and sleeping on) the books in Francesca's collection.

I could give a flying finch (as Dante would say) about reading. I watch television with Kate. When we were kittens, she barely knew a hundred words in Italian, but she learned by watching Italian game shows and *telenovelas* with me. I liked the Italian soap operas and the games were lively in a lowbrow way, but I really loved keeping up with the international news on Animal Planet and the BBC. That's where I perfected my English vocabulary.

"Come on, Dante," I pleaded. "Kate isn't coming home until after dinner with the stylish Stefano." Dante hated Stefano because he was grabby, both of cats and people, and he wore too much Hugo Boss cologne. "Stefano will probably come in for an hour or so." I was sealing the deal. I went in for the kill. "I'll take us over to Dante's House."

Dante Alighieri was a famous poet about eight hundred years ago. Dante, my brother, pontificated about his namesake *ad nauseam*. Francesca told me that I was named for Guido Cavalcanti, who was a friend of the original Dante and was also a poet. But I know that Dante the poet wasn't a true friend to Mr. Cavalcanti because, in his mean, petty, hurtful way, my brother informed me that Dante put his "friend" in one of the worst circles of hell in his really long, long, long poem that is entitled *The Divine Comedy*. But didn't seem so divine since poor Guido was in hell, or like a comedy because Guido wasn't laughing. Also, more to the point, Kate told me that I was named Guido because she thought the name was cute and I was a very cute kitten.

(Little did Kate know when she named me that when I turned two-years-old a bunch of embarrassing Guidos and Guidettes would be ruling a place called the Jersey Shore and she and I would be watching them on the television when Dante and Francesca weren't around to make fun of us.)

"Dante's House? You know how to get to the Dante Museum?"

"And Dante's Church," I added for extra points.

My brother looked very tempted. I could tell because he sat very very still and stared, blink-free, for what seemed like a whole minute.

"Tell me your plan," he said.

It took longer to explain the plan to Dante than it took to execute. I went first: 1) a jump from the terrace table to stone ledge of a boarded up window of the palazzo that formed the back wall of the gardens of both Gattone and Francesca; 2) a long leap (with no running room) from the ledge to low roof of our building (about four feet); 3) pause for breath; 4) scamper over terra cotta tiled roof; 5) ignore pigeons; 6) running start for five-foot leap to palazzo roof; and 7) gather to enjoy view.

When I made it to the first roof I stopped to watch Gattone. Dante came last. (I wasn't worried about him.) Gattone was already on the garden table, making ready for the jump to the ledge. The adventure adrenaline was clearly kicking in. He looked more like four-years-old than nine, a fat four, but also a frisky four. He sprang to the sill and flattened himself against the window so as not to fall back. He focused his blue eyes on me far above on the edge of the roof, crouched on his haunches and sprang.

Here we go again, I thought. He caught the edge of the curved terra cotta tiles with three paws. One hefty rear leg scrambled for purchase as he leaned forward and grabbed my leg with his teeth. The pain was intense, but lasted only a moment, when his back leg landed in the rain gutter and he pushed up and over me.

"No problem," he said. His pupils were huge and his chest pumped like an accordion playing a tarantella. "I'll just take a rest up here for a moment, if you don't mind."

I nodded, too concerned about my bruised spit-wet leg to comment. I repaired the damage with a couple of licks and didn't taste blood. No permanent harm.

By this time Dante had joined us, a bit miffed because neither of us watched his ascent. The three stripes on his forehead were drawn into one thick line. "Gattone, you know you will have to reverse the process on the way back."

"No problem," Gattone repeated. "I'm much better at going down. I always land on my feet." He took three more deep breaths. "Let's get this adventure under way." He bounded off to the left.

"Wrong way, Gattone," I called. "You're going to end up falling three stories into the street." He made a quick U-turn. "We're going over the roof of the bank and then down to Via del Corso. Along the way my brother can tell you every bit of history of the palazzo that houses the bank. You'll either puke or fall asleep."

"So sue me, I'm interested in history," said Dante. He brought up the rear again as we made running jumps to the bank's roof, which was identical with terra cotta tiles, but had a much better view in all directions than the top of our house.

As I predicted, Dante couldn't help himself. "The Banca Toscana may now own this great palazzo, but in 1260 it was owned by the Portinari family and they had a daughter named Beatrice. She was Dante Alighieri's great love." Dante tripped on a roofing tile and rolled into Gattone, probably because his eyes were looking eight-hundred-years into the past, instead of two seconds into the future. He didn't seem to notice. "My namesake probably looked up into the very windows of the Palazzo Portinari that we are sitting above, trying to catch a glimpse of his muse."

"Since they are long dead, might I suggest that you look back over your shoulder and take a gander at the best view in the whole city – the dome of the cathedral," I interjected.

Gattone literally gasped at the sight. "*Accidenti!* Look at that."

Dante, the tour guide droned on. "The dome was designed by Brunelleschi in the 1400s." But then he stopped, speechless at the view. There is no place from the apartments of Kate or Francesca that the dome could be seen. Even Gattone in his low garden couldn't see it. Our apartment building was only half a block from the cathedral, but captives that we were, we usually forgot it was there.

I must admit, I got great pleasure out of Dante and Gattone's awed expressions. I frequently climbed up on the roofs, so I've gotten used to how big the dome actually was. At the time, I thought this was going to be the moment Gattone would most remember out of the whole adventure. The sun was just starting to set so the dome glowed red and the gold ball at the very top seemed to be on fire.

Nothing in Florence was as tall as the dome, except for the tower on the city hall, but even the shorter Torre della Castagna, one block away from the Palazzo Portinari, cast a shadow over us. *We need to move along,* I thought. We didn't want to get locked out when the bank closed. Time to get down to the street. Also, I noticed a gray mountain of clouds rolling in from the east. Dante would freak out if it stormed.

"Hey, you two, we'll catch more of the view on the way back, let's get downstairs. We go this way," I said, as I led them over a metal walkway built on the roof, probably for viewing purposes, but evidently used by the smokers working in the bank, if the smelly butts were anything to go by. There was a narrow door propped open by a broken piece of roofing tile.

My nose told me there were no people around, so I slipped through to the top of a spiral staircase that hugged the corner of a huge room. A flaking fresco of a man on a horse and an angel sitting on a cloud above him covered the ceiling. An old painter's tarp lay bunched on the dusty floor. New white plaster snaked up the walls, patching some of the cracks. This place was certainly not as nice as our apartment, even though we could have fit our whole place into this one room. Nothing had changed since the last time I had scampered through there on a successful mouse-hunting mission a few nights before.

"Come on," I said. "Be really quiet and keep your ears cocked for footsteps." I led the way down the spiral staircase, raced across the room and into a narrow hall where another door led two stories down directly to the street. We hugged the wall, but it wasn't necessary. This deserted part of the palazzo was shut off from the bank. At the bottom was a closed door.

"How do we get out?" asked Dante, keeping an eye on the stairs behind us.

"We don't go out that door," I said. "It leads directly to Via del Proconsolo, a street that a bunch of buses and scooters use." Dante hated buses and the noisy Vespas even more. "We go through that grate." I put my forehead on a metal mesh over a cat-sized opening at the base of the stairs. It swung in on rusted hinges.

"I'm not going in there." Dante was also scared of small dark spaces. He probably thought his hefty rear would get caught.

"I will," said Gattone, diving through the opening. "If I fit through, you both will make it." His voice became more muffled as he crawled away. "Where does...end...?"

"You go next, Dante. There is room at the end for all of us. We'll be under the machine where people get money and behind a place where a lot of bicycles are parked."

Dante still wasn't convinced we should go on. "What happens if we get locked out of the bank or worse trapped inside on our way back home?"

"Brother, you can't let Gattone go on alone," I pushed him into the tunnel. "If we can't come back this way, we will go by the street. Our house is only a block away."

He tried to turn around, but the space was too small. "How do we get into our building?"

"Gaetano at the gelateria knows Gattone. He'll ring Giovanna. She'll open the door. We'll be in trouble, but we'll be home. I'm not stupid. I've thought of the contingencies."

I crawled out of the tunnel to find both cats licking dust and sand out of their fur. I waited until a lady wearing six-inch heels and snag-tempting fishnet stocking finished pulling money out of the wall right above our heads before I pushed open the grate and ran to hide among the bicycles. When we were all together, I held them back until a large group of Chinese tourists crossed Via del Corso and we mingled among their legs. Italians or Americans, and especially British people, would have noticed us and maybe even tried to catch us, but the Chinese just seem to think we belonged there. Also, I've observed on past excursions that speeding bicycles or scooters slow down for tour groups, but would flatten a cat in a second, without even pausing to check for signs of life.

We kept pace with the twittering Chinese because they were on their way to Dante's Church. We slunk through the doorway and hid under the last pew. We assumed that we were safe.

Gattone, of course, doesn't know how to behave in public; that is to be as quiet and invisible as possible. He wiggled his way out into the side aisle of the dark church. Probably nobody could see him, except Dante and me. I hoped so.

Our eyes worked very well in low light. The Church of Santa Margherita dei Cerchi, famed as Dante's Church, was the darkest in town. I heard Francesca explain to Kate one day that it was one of the few medieval churches that didn't get renovated in the Renaissance so there weren't any windows and the priest doesn't want to pay a high electric light bill. In fact, there was only one small spotlight that lands on a big stone on the altar. Now the stone was nothing special. I saw the fat priest (he looked something like the television actor who plays Agatha Christie's Poirot character) waddle in with the huge stone one day after swiping it from a pile the street crew dug up when they fixed the underground pipes. But he told everybody that he could see Dante's face in it. Since the priest claimed this was Dante's Church, I guess an ancient paving stone with the poet's face on it was, as they say, "suggestive."

I caught myself staring at the stone, so I missed the fact that Gattone was in danger of tripping some random tourist.

"Gattone, get back here," said Dante. "Someone is going to see you."

"Where is Beatrice's tomb?" Gattone threw the question over his shoulder as he continued along the aisle. Luckily, everyone who came in with us was still milling in the center of the church, listening to the Chinese guide chatter on and on.

"You do realize that she is not buried here," Dante, the expert on all things, said. "She died in childbirth when she was twenty-four and was buried in her husband's church, Santa Croce."

"But I see a tomb up there," Gattone said, as he came back to urge us forward.

Dante couldn't restrain his curiosity, but as he slunk ahead on his belly under the pews, he said, "It's not hers, no matter what it says. Francesca's history of the Portinari family said that Beatrice's father and nanny are buried here, but not her."

"Gattone, get under here. All of the tourists are heading this way," I hissed.

We huddled together under the bench right beside the tomb. There was a big basket almost full with little pieces of paper. One piece had missed the receptacle and lay at our paws.

"What does it say, Dante? " I said.

He anchored it with his left paw and spread it flat with his right. "Dear Beatrice," he read, "please look down from Paradise and intercede with my one and

only love, Harold. Make him realize that we are soul
mates, meant to be together for eternity, like you and
Dante. *Molte grazie*, Penny."

"That's sad," said Gattone.

"Well, Dante last saw Beatrice when she was
eighteen and they both married other people a year
later. So they may have been soul mates, but I bet
Beatrice never knew it until she got to Paradise." My
brother was a cynic when it comes to love. Being a
housecat in a building full of neutered tomcats had
that effect. I, on the other paw, got out more. I might
not be able to act on my love, but there was a little
calico cat who sat on a ledge down the street from us.
I made sure she knew my name. "Guidino, *tesoro*," she
called to me.

I was daydreaming again and missed the fact that
Gattone dived into the basket of love notes until
pounding feet just missed my whiskers. The smell of
dog stank up the place. Dante and I flattened
ourselves under the pew. Gattone was not so lucky.
All I saw was the tip of his tail as he flew out of the
basket. Literally flew. Only later did I realize that the
black-robed penguin of a priest had him by the scruff
of the neck.

"No cats in this church," he yelled. The same was
not the case for his rat-like dog. It was clear from the
odor that he got the run of the place. Luckily for
Dante and me that mongrel was at that moment
apparently sleeping off a heavy lunch in the nearby
rectory. It was the priest who stunk of dog. Sleep with
dogs, wake up with fleas, they say.

Storming to the door, swinging poor Gattone, whose legs were splayed, claws ready to catch onto anything, the priest flung him into the road. Dante and I took the diversion as a chance to race outside and up the two steps to the shop of the leather craftsman across from the church. His door was shut. We made ourselves as small as possible until the priest stomped back into Dante's Church.

We found Gattone halfway down the alley, almost at the door toward the Dante Museum. He was snuffling and licking and sniffing and mouthing his left back leg. "Ow, ow, ow, I think it's broken," he whimpered. "I flew so fast, too near the ground. No time to get all four paws down."

"Let me see," said Dante, licking his friend's ear. "I bet it's just bruised." He stuck his nose along the chubby leg. "There's no smell of blood or bone. Try to stand on it."

"Ow, ow, ow, well it may not be broken, but that dog-kissing priest does not show the love of St. Francis to all of God's creatures."

While the medical consultation went on, I took a couple of steps to the Dante Museum. Even if Dante's Church had been a failure, maybe we could recoup the day at the museum. More bad news, however, awaited us. The museum door was shut tight.

"Dante, come here, " I said. "Read that sign." A piece of paper fluttered in the breeze, attached to the door with a piece of tape.

"The Museum of Dante Alighieri is closed today at 5pm for maintenance." Just as he said this a big drop of rain hit my nose. Another drop splashed beside me, and then another and another.

"Bummer," I said, "so should we head for home?"

Dante gave me a "what the festering fur ball" look, but before he could speak an amplified voice that had the same American accent as Kate's, said, "The House of Dante is where the poet lived before his banishment in 1301."

"Baseless barnacles," my brother growled to me. "Dante didn't live here. This building was built in 1911 to create a museum dedicated to Dante. No one knows where Dante lived."

"Let's not get sidetracked. It's starting to rain," I said. Unfortunately I was so distracted by his rant about incompetent tour guides that I wasn't paying attention to the movement behind me until I got a whiff of dirty gym shoes and chocolate gelato. The gelato was on the sticky hands of a small redheaded boy who grabbed me about the stomach and held me aloft to his equally carrot-topped mother.

"Mummy, canna I keep him? He donna not have a collar." Irish or Scottish, I can never tell the accents apart, but it didn't matter. Outrage flowed through my body, my tail puffed in response.

"Liam, put that creature down."

Creature, I'll give you a creature, I thought, ready to mar that freckled nose for all eternity. But I didn't have to. My scaredy-cat brother lost his mind and sank his teeth into Liam's ankle. I was free. Both Liam and his mother screamed. Gattone, Dante and I raced around the corner of Dante's House, followed by the words, "Catch that cat. It probably has rabies or the plague. It bit my son."

This of course guaranteed that nobody touched us as we scampered across the street, through an open door and up two flights of wooden stairs.

The tower was tall and very dark. I realized immediately that we had escaped the sticky, smelly kid and his irate mother by ducking into the Torre della Castagna. Panting, we huddled together six flights up in the square stone tower. The only way out was the way we came in.

Down below a dim light glowed. A *vigile* blew his whistle and shouted in Italian, "Did they come in here, Alberto?"

"Who?" wavered a very old man voice.

"Three street cats."

"I didn't see anything. Nobody's been in all afternoon."

"Not people. Cats."

"Not a human, nor an animal, has come through that door, officer."

Of course the old man hadn't seen Dante, Gattone, or me. He was snoozing, head nested in his arms, as we raced past. I paused to look his way as we

scampered up the stairs because of the slight whiff I
caught of his left-over lunch, an anchovy, butter and
bread *panino*, half wrapped in white paper on the edge
of his desk. *If he goes back to sleep*, I thought, *I'm going
back for a snack*.

"Keep your door closed. Those cats may be
diseased. A British kid got bitten."

"One tourist more or less is not going to be
missed, officer."

"Can't comment on that, Alberto. Close the door.
It's going to pour down rain any second. It won't do
the collection any good." The door slammed behind
the policeman.

A shower of dust wafted down from above
where we were sitting. Gattone sneezed. Dante gave
him a bump with his head. "Lick your nose," he
whispered.

I always liked this tower. Many a warm afternoon
when Kate was out at her Advanced Italian class, I
would catch a few rays and fantasize about some fair
feline, either the cute calico down the street or a regal
Russian Blue like my sainted mother, being kept
prisoner high in the Torre della Castagna. I always
saved them from the evil Rat King and we lived
happily ever after with Kate. Sometimes I wondered
if Rapunzel was trapped in the tower how she would
manage to hang her braid of hair down the wall since
there were no windows.

"Let's go up a few more flights, Dante said,
breaking into my thoughts. "We've got to make a plan.
Kate is going to be home soon."

A crack of lightning and the roar of thunder told me we weren't going anywhere soon. Dante cowered in the corner of the landing, whimpering as the lightning flashed faster and the thunder boomed one on top of the next. I ordered Gattone to stay close to my brother as I went down to check out our situation (and to see if there was a snack left).

For seven flights down there were only dusty stairs and dustier landings marred by three sets of paw prints – small, medium and large. No light from below reached that height, but I could see enough with my extraordinary cat vision and the gray light coming through the square holes in the walls that were so thick not a drop of rain blew in.

I got down to where light filtered up the stairway. I went into slink mode, low on the steps, up against the wall. The walls were gray. Being also gray, I imagined myself invisible.

At about the tenth turn of the narrow staircase, the bare walls and dusty floors ended. Flags, tapestries, muskets, pikes, sabers, maps, and paintings covered the walls. Old wood cases with glass windows held pistols, books, faded photographs, old bits of paper scratched with ink, and so much other stuff that I can't remember, except for the old musty clothes: red shirts, red bandanas, blue wool button-up trousers with red stripes, and hats and caps, mostly red. (Dante would point out that our kind were color-blind, and couldn't see red, but I knew my reds, even though I don't see them like Kate does.)

Even when I looked down on the old man seated behind the desk, I couldn't see anything you would find in a normal apartment like Kate's. There wasn't a kitchen, or a bed, or any furniture except the old man's big desk and two chairs.

The photographs on the walls were mostly of one man with wild long gray hair, and matching beard and mustache. Personal grooming was clearly not one of Giuseppe Garibaldi's priorities. In pictures where he was older, he started to go bald on top, like Kate's boring boyfriend Stefano. Garibaldi wore a hat much of the time – a good idea for Stefano.

The man at the desk licked his fingers. All that was left of the anchovy and butter *panino* was crumbs and a delectable aroma. His cell phone rang. He wiped his hands on his slacks and answered it on the third chime. I didn't hear all of what he said, except "That's it for the today. I'm off to visit my sister in Rome for the week, since I don't have to be back here until I open next Thursday." He closed the phone, locked the drawer of the desk, straightened a bunch of brochures in the plastic box on the front edge, put on his coat and selected an umbrella from the stand by the door. In front of my horrified eyes, he opened the one and only door to the tower, put up his umbrella, stepped out, closed the door and locked it.

"Prisoners, That's what we are – prisoners." Dante was on the verge of yowling, not quite, but close.

"It's all my fault," said Gattone. "If I hadn't wanted an adventure, we wouldn't be stuck here."

Much as I would have loved to let Gattone take the blame, I hadn't called them to come down when it looked like the old man was leaving so that we could race out ahead of him. On the other paw, they probably would not have made it down in time. I also hadn't told them that the front door was closed until next Thursday, so they were anxious about getting into trouble with Giovanna and Kate, while I worried that we might not have food and water for a week and would surely perish.

Instead, I said, "This is not the fault of any of us. We are just victims of fate and an evil priest and a kid with sticky fingers. I still have chocolate on my fur and Gattone has a lame leg." I paused. "I'm just saying that we would be home by now if the adventure had run as we planned."

"Kate has to be back soon. She's going to worry," said Dante.

I gave Dante's ear a lick, trying to be soothing. He usually hates me doing that, but this time it seemed to help. "Remember she is out to dinner with the boyfriend. Then it will take her thirty minutes or so to figure out that we aren't across the landing at Francesca's place, longer if that idiot Stefano is with her."

"Roberto gets home when the Duomo bells ring seven times and that's when Giovanna feeds me. She will notice I'm gone when I don't come to eat. I'm very prompt," said Gattone, leaning against Dante. "She'll go crazy because she'd never think I might get outside the building. Unless, of course, I fell out of the front window...I did that once...trying to catch a pigeon. Four-footed landing, I must say."

Dante hid his head under both paws, past listening to me or Gattone. "How will they know where we are?"

I took a business-like tone. "They all will think we got out through the inside stairs and the street door to the building, maybe when the stair cleaner came or that the postman left the door open, like he sometimes does."

"All of us together?" Gattone seemed almost convinced.

"I'm not saying it makes sense. I'm just saying they will look for us out in the street and they will call for us and we will answer."

"Oh," said Dante, thinking hard, trying to find a flaw in my logic.

Not so with Gattone. "Guido, you are the smartest cat I know. You have it all figured out. Let's take turns listening for them calling us. I'll take the first nap." He turned one circle to the left and two to the right, tucked his nose under his paw and fell asleep.

I looked at Dante. He looked at me. We both looked at the sleeping Gattone.

"He doesn't realize that Kate, Giovanna and Roberto can't hear as well as we can and in this storm, they'll never figure out where we are," Dante said.

"Dante, they aren't going to give up after one try. The storm will end. They'll hear us and call the *vigili*."

"Or when they open the door to the Garibaldi collection tomorrow, we'll be ready to slip out."

I refrained again from telling Dante that the old man would not be back for seven days. By then it would not matter. I tried to distract him. "While we are waiting for Kate, tell me the story of our first rescue. Remember, we have been in worse spots than this, bro."

Dante almost smiled, but hid it by licking a paw and rubbing it over the ear where I had left my scent. He always seemed to hesitate before telling the story of our birth and the events that followed.

"We were born by the sea. Our mother was a feline Holly Golightly."

"What does that mean, Dante?"

"Read Truman Capote. She was a good-time girl, a cat of questionable morals."

I sat up, backed away, bumped into the snoring Gattone, who just wrapped his tail closer around his head. "You are not telling it *right*," I accused my brother. "Tell the real story."

"No I am telling the truth. Not making up some fairy tale for a rainy night. We are old enough to face the truth," said my brother in that holier-than-thou way he gets. "Look at the proof."

"What proof?" I said, choking on the words.

"We are both gray, but you are small, have spots, and yellow eyes. I am big, striped, and have green eyes. My fur is thicker and softer. Although that may be because I am a better groomer than you, I doubt it is the only reason. We clearly have the same mother because we were found in the same litter. But we have different fathers. If our sister had lived, she probably wouldn't have looked like either of us. Face it. Our mother had sex with every tomcat on the beach."

The fur on my neck rose. My tail puffed out. "Take that back," I cried. "Mother was a royal Russian Blue. Those toms, if there was more than one, took advantage of her. She must have been accidentally locked out of her villa by the sea. Probably by the family cook or maid. That's the story I want you to tell."

"You just hate the idea that she abandoned us in that trash bin on purpose," Dante said as he stared me down and I blinked. "Look at the facts. We were found in a big metal garbage container behind a fish restaurant on the boardwalk of Forte dei Marmi."

I interjected, "Forte dei Marmi is where all of the Russian billionaires have their summer villas. I'm sure our mother still lives in one of them and misses us every day. She probably flies back and forth to

Moscow on the family plane and each time she gets to the villa, she looks for us."

Dante ignored me. "Back to the facts. We were found in a garbage bin. Fact. We were alone. Fact. There was another kitten, a girl, our sister. Fact. She was dead. Fact. Our eyes weren't even open so you never saw the cat that gave birth to us. All we know about her is that she had short hair. She may have even been Siamese because you like to talk and have a whiny voice. You also have a crook in your tail, the same as many Siamese, but that could have come from your father for all we know. Russian Blues have green eyes. Yours are yellow."

I chewed at the right-angled bone at the end of my tail and didn't say anything whiny. I always wanted green eyes, like Dante.

"We were maybe two days old, no older. Luckily it was a warm April, by the sea or we would have died, too."

I made one more plea. "But I'm sure. I know in my bones that our beautiful mother gave birth to us in a quiet corner of the villa. I remember her tongue washing me for the first time. I remember her purr. I bet the evil cook grabbed us up and put us in that bin because it was clear that we were not of noble blood, like our mother. Our mother would not have abandoned us, just like Kate won't abandon us."

"Kate may have no choice because of this bonehead adventure of yours. Our flighty mother had a choice. She got pregnant, she gave birth among a bunch of fish heads, used napkins and placemats, and then went on her merry way."

"No, no, no, no," I yowled at him. "She had no choice. She loved us, but that billionaire Russian couldn't tolerate mixed-breed cats wandering around the villa. He probably told the evil cook to get rid of us."

"Pure fantasy, Guido," Dante purred, his eyes narrowed as he watched my pain. "Let's get back to facts. We were found in the garbage. Fact. We never knew who found us, but they turned us over to a feline protection group in Prato, near to Florence. Fact. We were put in a foster home run by Lucia and Gino. Fact.

"I remember Lucia. She had the warmest, softest hands," I said, calming down a bit.

"Yes she did," said Dante, letting me relax before jabbing at me again. "She told us about our dead sister."

I refused to think ugly thoughts. "She fed us every three hours, night after night. She rubbed us and helped us to learn to poo and pee."

Dante nodded, looking out the small square window into the veil of rain. "Otto helped, too. Usually a good mother cat, who does not abandon her kits, licks them all over, even their private parts."

"I remember. I remember," I said, getting excited. "Lucia, held us for Otto to lick."

"Being a dog and worse, a hunting hound, a dachshund, it's amazing Otto didn't have us for a snack."

"But instead he just licked us all over making sure our tummies worked right," I remembered. "I will always have a soft spot for dogs because of Otto."

"Actually, I think you caught some dog from him. You're so needy, always following Kate around, constantly asking to be petted." Dante gave me a piecing look. "You need to learn to be more aloof, like me. Then you won't have this fear of abandonment."

"Who are you, a pet therapist?"

"I'm just saying that with dogs it is always good to do as the Russian proverb says, 'Trust, but verify' and be ready to run like hell," said Dante. "Never trust a dog you don't know."

"Except for the scrawny, yapping dog of the priest, I've never met another dog, except Otto," I said.

Dante got distracted from his story. "What was up with that priest? I've seen him a dozen times from our window when he takes bags of donated change to the *ortolano* on the corner. I never thought he could be so angry to throw poor Gattone against a wall."

"Gattone did jump into his basket of Beatrice messages. He must make a lot of money off of the Dante and Beatrice fans."

"But that's no excuse to use violence. He could have said 'scat' and Gattone would have run."

Even in his sleep Gattone must have heard his name. He raised his head and said, "What are you jabbering about?"

I gave him a pat on the head with a paw. "Dante is telling the story of how we were saved from certain death by Kate."

"Kate saved you? I thought she just offered to let you live with her. That's what she told Giovanna. She said she was tired of sharing me with them and wanted a kitten or two. I tried not to feel rejected, but I did." Gattone had trouble keeping his eyes open.

"That's saving isn't it? If she hadn't offered to let us share her apartment we would have been abandoned to our fate." I tried to make Gattone feel better about us edging him out.

Dante didn't see it that way. He batted me about the ears. "Cut the drama queen act. Kate came to see the foster kittens at Lucia and Gino's house. She picked us. Lucia checked her out and approved her request. Lucia would have never abandoned us. The worst thing that might have happened is that we would have gone to separate homes, which might not have been a bad thing. I always wondered what it would have been like to be an only cat."

"That's mean, Dante," said Gattone.

"I would have been fine with Kate, without you." I huffed out a breath, wanting to make a rude gesture, but not knowing how.

"She would have returned you after the first day. Remember? You vomited in the carrier all the way home on the bus."

"The fact that she didn't return me just shows how much more she loves me than you. She would never leave me."

"You need therapy, Guido. Abandonment issues and a decided lack of irony. All cats *get* irony. You can't take a joke. You *must* be a dog."

"Uh, guys," said Gattone. "You might want to shut up."

"Don't worry, buddy," said Dante. "We're just having a little fun."

"No, I mean, you might want to stop talking. I think I hear Kate calling."

"Dante. Guido. Kitty, kitty, kitty." Kate called from somewhere far below our perch. She sounded a bit frantic, which is understandable since it was still storming.

"Can you see her? Can you see her?" Dante moved from frantic to hysterics as he tried to squeeze himself into one of the square openings in the wall. The tower wall was so thick that he got half way to the outside edge and became stuck. He pushed back. "Guido, you try. I bet you can see out. Call to her."

I crept all they way out and took a quick look down. We were much further up from the street than I first imagined. Lightning flashed and I saw her. My darling Kate. Her blond ringlets plastered to her head. Why wasn't she carrying an umbrella? Where was that idiot Stefano?

"Is she there?" shouted Dante.

"Yes, but she is a block away on Via del Corso. Even though her ears are bigger than yours, she will never hear me."

"Try anyway," he ordered.

I yowled my loudest. "*MEOURRLOORRU, MEOURRLOORRUU.*" It's the call I usually save to announce the triumphant capture of a tasty bat or mouse, but sometimes I use it when Kate goes out the door with a suitcase and I don't know if she is every coming back, even though I know Francesca and Giovanna will feed Dante and me. Kate told me once that she heard this yowl from the street door three floors down and that it always ruins the first day of her vacation. *Good. Mission accomplished*, I thought at the time.

She was much farther away and it was raining and a scooter went by. She didn't even turn her head in my direction.

"We have to go to her," I said to the others as I backed out of the window hole. "She's going to get sick looking for us in the rain. She might get pneumonia. She might die." I had pneumonia when I was a kitten and I almost died, except Kate gave me medicine and kept me with her for a whole week, day and night, until I felt better.

"But it's raining, " said Gattone.

"But the door is locked," said Dante.

I insisted. "This is an ancient tower. Dante, you told me that it was built to defend a family, like to Montalets."

"Capulets and Montagues," he corrected.

"Whatever. The point is that there must be an escape hole or door or something because those people weren't stupid. There might even be one of these small windows down lower that I can squeeze through and jump down and go get Kate. She can get the vigili to let you two out."

"I say that we wait until the old man comes back tomorrow," said Gattone. "We'll run out when he comes in and it won't be raining and we won't get wet."

"Umm, I guess I failed to mention," I mumbled. "He's not coming back for a week. The museum or collection or whatever this is only open on Thursdays."

"*What?*" Dante turned on me with a horrified look in his eyes. "Why are we sitting here, wandering down memory lane, wasting precious time when we should be looking for a way out."

"We were waiting for Kate and Giovanna," I reminded him.

"Freakin' feline, they *can't* hear us, so they *aren't* coming. Let's go." Dante ran headlong down the stairs. I kept pace with Gattone who still limped. I hoped that Dante would cool off by the time we reached the bottom. He was liable to take a swipe at my ear.

All of the lower venting holes had been blocked with cement. There was only one exit door and another closed door to a toilette, if the odor in that corner was anything to go by. That corner had been squared off with plywood sometime in the last century. Dante was fond of telling me how disgusting the medieval people were because they didn't cover their waste; they just threw it into the street.

Gattone, propped up against the toilette door, watching as Dante and I searched behind the flags and tapestries and maps for some sort of opening. We couldn't find an escape route.

"Hey, that's a nice breeze," said Gattone. "It makes my leg feel better. I bet I need to ice the bruise. Or is heat better?"

"What are you driveling on about, Gattone?" I said. "Can't you see we're busy here?"

"What breeze?" Dante rushed over to our neighbor. "There aren't any windows here."

"It's coming from under the door," said Gattone. "It doesn't smell so good, but it feels real nice."

I gave Gattone a shove. "If there is air moving then there's a hole." I jumped at the latch and missed.

"Let me," said my brother. He stretched his whole length up the door and got one paw over the lever and dragged it down. The door opened.

The room was tiny. Just a seatless toilet and a sink. But in the center of the floor was a large metal grate. The three of us strained to see what was below. It was a large black hole.

Luckily for us, the floor had been leveled with concrete so that the grate could be securely attached and near the toilet the concrete had sloughed off down into the deep hole.

"It's the escape tunnel," Dante said. "Can you get through, Guido?"

"No, problem," I said, "but we don't know how deep it is or what is at the bottom."

"You got us here, you check it out," said my unsympathetic brother.

Gattone tested the opening with his head. "I think we can all get through. My whiskers don't touch on the sides so it's wide enough and I can get my head in. Usually if an opening meets both criteria, I can flatten myself enough to squeeze through."

"Guido, go under and check out the situation. If you can get back up, then scrape off some of the dirt under the cement and widen the hole. Then, we will try to get in." Dante paced back and forth.

I don't know why I was taking orders from my brother, but he was so calm (except for the pacing), I thought I should humor him. I slipped under the grate, flipped on my stomach and dug my claws in. I slid about three feet. The opening was large enough for a small person and best of all when the tunnel straightened out there was no water running in it.

I went back to the top and dug with all of my might, getting filthy in the process. Soon Gattone and Dante were on my side of the grate and we escaped the tower. Only to be trapped underground.

"Do you see how the packed dirt has ended and now it is soft stone?" my brother, the geologist, said.

"Huh?" I said.

"It's tufa stone. It's under the whole city. People created caves to store wine and food under their houses in this stone. Florence is built on a bunch of natural and man-made caves. Francesca showed me a book about how the Romans built the first fort for a garrison here and all of the buildings have been covered by layers of medieval buildings that were covered by Renaissance buildings. Layers and layers of history."

I didn't care about the history or what kind of rock we were trapped in. I wondered which way we were going. We had covered about one hundred feet and there was no light in front of us and no light behind.

"I smell incense," said Gattone.

"I only smell dirt," I said.

"I smell Gattone," said Dante who brought up the rear. "Giovanna is going to give you a bath tonight, old friend."

I kept thinking Dante was way too cheerful for the situation.

"I don't care so long as I get dinner with the bath," said Gattone, "but I still smell incense."

"How do you know what incense smells like?" I asked.

"Giovanna took me to be blessed at the San Lorenzo church on the feast day of Saint Francis when I was two and not as heavy to carry across town. The young priests in robes were waving around things on sticks that had burning incense inside them."

"I smelled incense in Dante's Church," I said. "Maybe this escape route comes out in the church. If you were running from your enemies in medieval times, maybe the church is the closest safe haven."

"Is it lighter up ahead?" Gattone was looking over my back.

I couldn't see any difference, but I still had dust in my eyes from the excavation.

Dante must have been able to see around Gattone. "Yes, I think it is. Hurry up, Guido."

I picked up the pace and sure enough we came to an opening along one side of the tunnel. An opening covered by thick wire mesh. Through the screen we could see marble boxes and plaques with writing carved into them.

"Dante, what does that say?" I pointed at a big square gray marble box with carved writing on the side.

"It's in Latin."

"So? Translate it." I was impatient. Dante was just making the point that he can read Latin.

"I can't see all of it, but the essence is that in the box are the bones of Folco Portinari. That's Beatrice's father."

"And over there?" I stuck my nose through the mesh at flat slab.

"Somebody named Cerchi is buried there. You know the real name of Dante's Church is Santa Margherita de'Cerchi. I bet we are beside the crypt."

"What's a crypt?" said Gattone.

"Where all the bodies are buried."

"Maybe we'll see Beatrice's tomb," Gattone said.

Dante impatiently moved on. "I told you. She's not here. She was buried with her husband's family, the Bardi, in Santa Croce. Once a girl was married off, she never came home."

"But if it's Dante's Church, why isn't Dante buried here?"

"That's too long of a story to tell. We have to find a way out," Dante said. "Guido keep going. I feel as if the gravestones are whispering to me."

I agreed. The place was creeping me out. There wasn't a smell of recent death but the mix of marble, bone, and decaying fabric, with the hint of incense made me a little nauseous. The metal mesh ended at the edge of the cave-like room and the tunnel curved around it. Just then I saw light, dim and flickering. Unfortunately, I also heard voices.

There were ten steps cut into the tufa stone about twenty feet in front of us as we sat on the floor of the tunnel trying to tune in on the conversation above. We were under the altar of Dante's Church, at the end furthest from the door. I couldn't hear any noise from the alley, so I thought the door was probably closed.

Two men were talking. One was the evil priest who had thrown Gattone out of the church just hours before. Worse than the sound of the two men talking, I could hear the long nails clicking on the stone floor as the priest's ugly dog paced back and forth. He wasn't worth much as a dog, I thought, because he hadn't caught the scent of three dirty cats right below his nose.

"This is a genuine fifteenth century piece," the priest was saying. I could imagine him like a black toad in his cassock, although maybe he was in his after-hours clothes of rumpled corduroy trousers and a sweater with patched elbows. I'd seen him from our apartment window walking toward the trattoria on the corner in his off-duty clothes. Once I tried to spit on his head. I missed him, but I got the dog. The mutt was so stupid. He didn't even glance up.

"It's harder to get them out of the country these days," said the other voice, a man with the accent of somebody from Venice.

"This is so small, but valuable, it shouldn't be a problem," the priest said. "I'm having a copy made. It should be done in a week."

The conversation was apparently starting to disturb Dante because he slipped into what I liked to call "ghost cat" mode and he slunk up the stairs. Not to seem frightened, I followed. Gattone was probably smartest, by staying put, but, of course, he had been on the wrong end of an exchange with the priest earlier.

Sure enough, we were behind the altar. We used it as cover. The spotlight on the paving stone had been turned off. The only light in the church came from a bank of ten or twelve little candles left by those who came to say prayers to Santa Margherita or perhaps to entreat Beatrice on a love matter.

The portly priest and a tall skinny man in a raincoat were standing by the door. The scraggly dog paced back and forth faster and faster, like he needed to go for something called "walkies." From the window of our apartment the week before, I'd heard the priest say to him, "Got to go for walkies, *tesoro*? Time for walkies?" Embarrassing.

Holding a carved wooden angel in his left hand and gesturing with his right, the priest said, "It's part of a pair. If you can get me a good price on this one I can give you the other by the end of the month. Got to get a copy made of it, too."

"He's selling the church's art," whispered Dante.

"So what? He's the priest. It's his church," I said.

"No, he's just charged with taking care of it. He doesn't own it. He's stealing."

"I don't care right now. I just want us to be ready when they leave. They've got to leave. They don't live here."

"Right. Right. First things first," said Dante. "Go get Gattone. We have to get close to the door."

I slipped back down the steps and murmured to Gattone. He followed me up the stairs. The three of us slipped up the aisle toward the still-full Beatrice basket. We were halfway to the front when the priest yelled.

"Not on the floor, you idiot. Outside." He threw open the door and pushed the dog out into the rain.

We froze. *Please, please, please don't let them leave, yet,* I sent a strong message to Beatrice Portinari. And it worked. The priest closed the door.

"How much," he said.

"I can probably get a couple of thousand from either a Russian or Chinese client of mine."

"A couple of thousand? Not good enough. Ten at least."

"I might be able to do fifteen for the pair. If they are matched."

I nudged Gattone and Dante toward the back pew. It seemed to me like negotiations were coming to a close.

At that moment, the priest opened the door with the words "Fifteen thousand and not a euro less."

It all happened at once. I gave Gattone a shove and Dante and I were right on his tail. We raced out the door causing the priest to slip and crash into the tall man who stepped on my crooked tail causing me great agony, but that didn't slow us down.

We were out in the rain with a wet dog doing his business on the pavement. He couldn't stop mid-stream so we had a head start and outpaced him all the way out of Via Santa Margherita, left on Via del Corso and an immediate right on Via dello Studio, straight to our front door. Luck was still with us because Gaetano had the door to the gelateria open and we skidded inside. And who was there? Kate! Her hair was a mess, but I didn't care because she gathered me up to her shoulder and after patting Dante and Gattone on their heads, she gave me the biggest hug.

I figured the love fest would last about five minutes before we got to see the very angry mother side of her. But that was okay with me.

Dante and I didn't remember the stolen angel until days later. Did we do something about it? Yes, we did. But that is the subject of another tale...

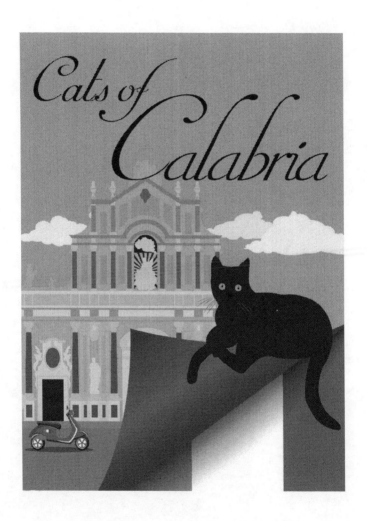

CATS OF CALABRIA:

Vanda, Uffa and Pussipu

Vanda lapped up the last of the milk from the blue and yellow ceramic bowl. Catching the final drip off her whisker with a small pink tongue, she padded across the terracotta floor to the only square of sunlight in the room to begin her morning spit bath.

I am the luckiest cat in the world, she thought midway through licking her left leg from haunch to paw. Her friend Pussipu lived in a much more luxurious house on the hill overlooking the valley, but all that pampered pussy got to drink was water with her meals. Vanda lived at a dairy, a water buffalo dairy to be precise, where the best *mozzarella di bufala* in Calabria was made. She got a bowl of milk every morning and every evening, the richest milk on earth.

The food wasn't bad, either. This southern Italian region was famed for its fried calamari, sardines under olive oil, thick lasagna, and spicy salami. Vanda didn't get to taste any of those dishes – the Vacarini family, who cared for her, fed her only dry kibble – but the farm had a never-ending supply of mice, voles, lizards and on her peppiest days, birds. In the springtime, the abundant litters of rabbits made a nice dietary change of pace. Having to chase down her snacks kept Vanda in shape.

She ran her tongue down her sleek black tail, nipping at an itch near the base. Vanda was completely black except for one white paw, which she used to emphasize her point in any argument. Her fur was short, making it easy for her to maintain its glossy sheen, except on the day of her monthly dust bath.

A long-legged teenager pushed through the rainbow-colored rope door curtain, bringing a flash of sunshine and fresh morning breeze. "Vanda, there you are," said Angelica Vacarini. "I have your new flea collar." She squatted down by the cat, her skirt billowing out around them. "I noticed yesterday that you were starting to itch and scratch." She unbuckled the old faded blue collar, slid off the tiny heart-shaped i.d. medallion, and transferred it to the new collar before attaching it to Vanda's neck. "With this green one you are going to be very stylish."

Vanda rubbed the side of her mouth and cheek over Angelica's hand, leaving a tiny mark of scent that said, *This is my person*. Angelica was just ten when her Uncle Zino brought a small black kitten to her birthday party.

"You have to get out of the shop soon. It's almost time for Signora Esmeralda to make her weekly stop for a *burrata* or two and a *treccia grande*. She does love that braided mozzarella, but she doesn't appreciate the fact that you are the cleanest cat in all of Calabria. She doesn't think cats belong inside, anywhere. Actually, I don't think she believes cats should exist at all." Angelica peered out the window to see who was beeping their car horn. "Hurry now. That's her Fiat 500 coming down the road."

Vanda didn't mind getting out of the Caseificio Torre Mordillo shop. Signora Esmeralda was bad tempered and smelled of unwashed cocker spaniel. It was also time for her self-appointed rounds.

The black cat loped across the dusty parking lot to a long stone building that housed the metal milking stalls, empty by mid-morning, the concrete floors still wet where Berto, the handyman, had hosed them down. It was the best place to have a game of mouse pong when an unwary critter came out for a sip of water.

Her next stop was the huge low-roofed barn, redolent of dung, with its muddy paddocks that edged up to the pond. Vanda expected the barn and the expanse of muck to be unoccupied unless one of the older water buffalos, like Peppa or Nerina, was

taking a prolonged mud bath. Now that it was
September, the herd usually cooled off in the pond in
the afternoon.

Most likely all of the girls would be out eating
grass and chewing the cud in the small pasture on the
other side of the pond. There weren't any calves. The
four heifers, one tawny, three umber black, born
seven months earlier, were almost grown. They
brought the herd up to twelve total. The three boy
calves had recently been sold off to a ranch in
Basilicata. *Out of sight, out of mind,* thought Vanda.

She wove her way through the tall dry grass of
the pasture. The water buffalos paid no attention to
her. Water buffalos didn't talk much and she didn't
understand what little they did say, anyway. In a
couple of months the grass would be gone and they
would be fed hay back at the barn.

Her tour was finished. It was time for her first
nap of the day. She walked the wooden planks atop
the pasture fence back to the barn. On her way across
the parking lot, Vanda saw Signora Esmeralda come
out of the shop carrying two string totes. Mozzarella
swimming in salt water could be seen in three
knotted-off clear plastic bags inside the thin cotton
sacks.

Vanda swerved to circle behind the store to
check on the workshop in the back. She leapt to a
high window sill. Inside was a white-tiled room – the
only place on the property Vanda was not allowed to
enter – where the mozzarella magic happened. As she

watched Angelica's father at work, her eyes began to close.

Pussipu felt out of sorts. She sat on her big brocade pillow with its gold tassels, placed in the huge picture window of the villa's *sala grande*. With brooding orange eyes, she scanned the broad expanse of the green and yellow valley that opened out to a rocky plain. Next came the village and after the port, the sea. A morning haze sat low on the water. It would lift by mid-day, she knew.

After a few deep breaths – Pussipu practiced mindfulness – she pinpointed the source of her discontent. The Bad Man, Don Pino, had been in the house last night. She could still smell his Versace Eros aftershave and the black Turkish cigarettes he smoked, one after another. Worse, he had run his hand down her back before she could wake and flee to the kitchen. After hours of grooming, she still hadn't been able to get the stink out of her long fur.

It had also been a sleepless night for her beloved Tommaso and his mother Amelia. Don Pino had harangued Tommaso without end from the time he entered the villa until he left near midnight. Pussipu could only remember the words *famiglia, 'Ndrangheta, locale, Quintino, responsabilità* and *picciotti d'onore*. There were also many mentions of Don Leopoldo, Tommaso's father, who had died the year before

Pussipu was born. Talk of her husband's death frightened Amelia Zacari and angered Tommaso.

Pussipu's mother, Petalosa, once told her daughter that she was in the same room with Don Leopoldo when he was shot with the same kind of gun used to kill the feral dogs that traveled in packs in the nearby hills. Petalosa never forgot the roar of the gun or the blood on the walls and floor of the villa's cantina. Don Pino had been there that horrible day, Petalosa recounted.

Pussipu was born in the spring after the murder. Tommaso was only eleven and soon became her constant companion. Her mother, an old cat, had died a few years later. Pussipu was now ten.

The evening before, Tommaso kept protesting that he wanted to return to medical school at Sapienza University in Rome. Don Pino insisted that Tommaso owed the family his loyalty and presence in Poggio dei Zacari. Long after Don Pino roared off in his red Ferrari, Tommaso paced the halls of the villa. Signora Amelia stayed in the kitchen cooking *ribollita*, *popettone* and *tiramisu*. Signora Amelia always cooked when she was distressed.

When her people were awake, Pussipu could not rest. Lack of sleep made her very grumpy. The morning sun was high in the sky and it was now quiet except for Tommaso snoring softly as he lay stretched out on the long couch, but still the Persian cat could not relax.

Signora Amelia hadn't been to bed, but she had quit cooking and started cleaning. Tommaso woke when she steered the vacuum cleaner down the hall. He began to pace again. It was all too tense for Pussipu. She decided to visit her friend Vanda at the dairy in the valley. Maybe she could center herself at the farm. Nothing ever happened there.

By the road it was many miles from the villa on the hill to the farms on the valley floor, but by cat path it was just over a thirty minute stroll. Pussipu did not allow herself to be distracted by a small brown snake that slithered out from under the rose bush or the squirrel that chattered from the big oak tree outside the villa's front gate. At one point she got a whiff of a mark left by Pasquale, the tomcat who roamed the area looking for food or love, or both.

By the time she turned down the lane at the Caseificio Torre Mordillo she was already in a better frame of mind.

Angelica's mother Delia came out of the house as the chocolate brown Persian rounded the corner. "Pussipu," she said, "how are you doing this morning?"

Pussipu blinked her large orange eyes, narrowing them with the pleasure of seeing one of her favorite people. She amped up the greeting, winding in and out of Delia's legs while purring.

"Did you come to visit Vanda?" Delia held open the door. "She just settled down for a nap, but I'm sure she will rouse herself for you … at least for a moment or two." Delia chuckled and closed the door once the fluffy cat crossed the threshold.

Pussipu knew that Vanda napped in any of three places: on Angelica's bed, in the window seat of the kitchen or behind Roberto Vacarini's laptop. She could hear him typing, so that was the most likely spot.

In a small office adjacent to the kitchen, Roberto was working on invoices for Caseificio Torre Mordillo's shipments of *mozzarella di bufala* that went out by van three times a week to fine restaurants in Calabria and as far away as Sorrento. Three- and four-star restaurants used only the best *mozzarella di bufala* to layer a *caprese* salad or to stuff zucchini blossoms before frying or to shred over pasta with crushed tomato or on pizzas cooked in wood-burning ovens.

The mozzarella from Torre Mordillo was of the highest quality because Roberto treated his water buffalo with respect. It was his belief that only a happy animal could provide the quality milk necessary for exceptional mozzarella.

He was lucky because the valley had no heavy industry, incinerators or refuse landfills. So much of southern Italy had polluted groundwater, the same water in which the buffalo bathed and the well water they drank. Mozzarella made at dairy farms near Naples tested positive for dioxin.

Pussipu sat at Roberto's feet, but when he didn't notice her presence she placed her paws on his right knee and extended her claws – just a little bit.

"*Accidenti!* Pussipu, no need to do that!" Roberto poked the sleeping Vanda. "Take your friend out of here. I have work to do."

Vanda yawned, stretched her hind quarters high and walked across the keyboard.

"Vanda, you deleted my total." Roberto grabbed her around the middle and set her on the floor next to Pussipu. "Scat, the two of you."

"My work is done," said Vanda, touching noses with her friend. "Let's check out the kitchen. The sun should be coming through the window. I'm still thinking of finishing my nap. Want to join me?"

"Of course, but first let me tell you what happened up at the villa last night."

Vanda sprang up on the seat under the window bay. It was upholstered in a jungle print cotton depicting a variety of parrots. She was waiting for the day a real parrot would fly into her valley.

The shutters were drawn against the midday sun, except for the one on the far left windowpane. Knowing Vanda liked a sunbath, Delia left the shutter open to allow the sunlight to warm the cushion. The black cat turned in a circle and settled in for a chat. Pussipu joined her in the sun, tucking her front paws under her chest.

"I'm worried about Tommaso," she started. "Don Pino – the Bad Man – was at the villa last night. He's trying to make Tommaso do something he doesn't want to do."

"Like what?"

"I don't know. Things are always more complicated up at the villa. Not like here where there are only nice people, buffalo, milk and cheese and lunch … speaking of lunch is that *fileja alla tropeana* and *spinache e ceci con le sarde* that I smell? I love the sardines, but sometimes the onions are a bit strong for my delicate tummy."

"Can't miss the sardines and spinach aroma," Vanda patted the other cat on her ears with her white paw. "But you know I never get anything prepared for me, like Signora Amelia does for you. What did you have for breakfast?"

"A bit of *polpettone*, some liver pâté and a couple of fresh anchovies."

"Like I said."

"And a sliver of *branzino* from the whole fish she grilled for Don Pino last evening. They didn't finish it because of the fight." Pussipu got up. "It's all the negative energy at the villa. It's so tense. You know how I need good vibrations for my meditation. How can I be in the moment when Tommaso is pacing and Amelia is vacuuming, mopping and scrubbing?"

"You should do what you always tell me to do. Breathe. In. Out. In. Out. Maybe I can get a short nap in while you are getting yourself in the Zen zone."

An hour later, after Delia arrived to finish lunch preparations for the family, Vanda and Pussipu strolled off up the track through the scrub brush and olive groves toward the villa.

"Have you seen Pasquale lately?" Vanda asked.

"Funny you should ask. I thought I smelled his spritz on a fence post on my way down this morning." Pussipu stopped to get her bearings. "Up there it was." She batted at a yellow-spotted lizard that skittered across the path. "He is not welcome up at the villa. I get locked up tight when he's around or anytime I'm feeling amorous, if you know what I mean." She winked.

"I understand perfectly. Unfortunately I never feel romantic, so I only see Pasquale when they are harvesting hay and he comes over to see if he can catch a bunny or two."

"Did I hear my name?" From on top of a boulder to their right a pair of rakish yellow eyes glinted out of an orange tiger-striped face, its symmetry ruined by a scar over one brow and a ragged left ear.

"Pasquale, you old rogue," exclaimed Pussipu. "Are you spying on us?"

The huge tomcat stretched and clambered down the rock. "Would I do that? Nope, we were just fated to meet today, my lovelies." He looked over his shoulder. "I was waiting for a lady."

"We're ladies," said Vanda.

"A *younger* lady," he said, sticking his head into a flowering myrtle spurge bush. "Come out, my little fluff ball. They're friends."

A bashful young calico cat peered through the gray-green prickly leaves.

"Let me introduce Uffa."

"Uffa? What kind of name is *Uffa?*" Pussipu struck her most regal pose, a frown forming over her flat nose.

"It's a delectable name. Uffa. Uffa Uffa." Pasquale gave the word his most sexy purr at the same time that Uffa said, "It's the kind of name given when high spirits and clumsiness meet in one cat." She looked back and forth between the two female felines. "Of course, I expect to get more graceful … someday."

"So your humans keep huffing '*uffa*' when you get on their nerves," observed Vanda. "Like '*Uffa*, give me some peace' or '*Uffa*, don't eat that' or '*Uffa*, get out of here.'"

"Sort of…"

Pussipu interrupted, "You are clearly too … uh … naïve … to be hanging out with Pasquale."

"Um…," Vanda started, looking between the tomcat and the young cat. "I think another '*uffa*' moment has already happened. Knowing Pasquale, it didn't take long."

"Hey," Pasquale protested.

"I sure hope you didn't let him take advantage of you." Pussipu took a whiff near Uffa's tail before leaping back a foot. "*Bambina*, how could you?"

Vanda turned on Pasquale with a growl, swiping at his nose with her white paw. "What? The sisters who live behind the fish restaurant aren't enough in the romance department for you? You have to take advantage of a missy who's clearly lost?"

"Hey, hey, hey … she's an adult," he sputtered, but couldn't meet the black cat's eyes. "And I *did* promise to show her home."

"So, I'm right, you do have a home?" Pussipu asked and then answered her own question. "Of course you do. You're not all beat up, like this old hairball. Instead of smelling like rotting mice, you have some sort of perfume. What is that? Not a spice, but…"

"It's licorice," said Uffa. "I live at the licorice factory in the village near the sea."

"Licorice? Like the plant?" Vanda sniffed Uffa's neck.

She nodded. "That's how I got stuck up here. I was sleeping in the back of the foreman's truck when he decided to come up to see if there was any late harvest licorice root to be gathered. I was exploring when he drove off."

"You must have been in the fields in the next valley over," said Vanda. "I saw them pulling up the roots there last spring."

Pussipu's stomach growled. "Time for me to be getting back to the villa."

"I'd be happy to walk with you, *Principessa*." Pasquale rubbed up against the Persian cat.

"Get away from me, you smelly tom. You've had enough action today. Tommaso will turn the hose on you if he sees you. Go with Vanda and Uffa. You two should be able to find the licorice factory for the *gattina*."

Vanda didn't let them get more than five minutes down the path before she sent Pasquale on ahead.

"Sorry, *ragazzo*, but you are *rank*. All those male pheromones are overpowering the lovely smell of wild sage and rosemary." She sat in the middle of the track, blocking Uffa's way. "Let's let him get a good head start. We can't fail to follow his lead."

Uffa took the time to give herself a quick tongue bath. "Please tell me I don't stink of him. I just lost my wits back there." She hung her head. "He's such a charmer."

Vanda nodded. "In a 'here today, gone tomorrow' kind of way." She licked behind Uffa's ear, the places she couldn't reach. "You still smell more of licorice than Pasquale. It's nice."

"That's because the mice I dine on every day eat the licorice root. I'm licorice inside and out."

"Is that why they let you live at the factory?"

Uffa followed the path downhill. "It used to be me and my brothers and our mother. We were so good at our jobs that the supply of mice started running low. My brothers wandered off to the fishing port. Once you have a taste for fish, you don't go back to mice."

"Does your mother still live with you?"

"Unfortunately she was flattened by a speeding delivery truck." She heard Vanda's quick intake of breath. "Now it's just me and I'm finding it hard to keep the pests under control."

"Do you have a human to look out for your interests? At the dairy I have Angelica, Delia and Roberto. I only have to catch mice if I want to keep up my hunting skills."

"The owner of the factory, Signora Della Spagna, likes our kind well enough and she appreciates the work that I do. She instructed the night watchman to fill a metal bucket with fresh water every morning for me before he leaves. He mostly remembers. There's also one of the girls who works on the packing line who eats her lunch outside. She feeds me salami from her panino. She brushes me and talks to me about what's happening in the factory."

"You don't get to go inside?"

"They say that cat hair in the licorice drops wouldn't be a good idea, but sometimes I take a tour of the cooking room. It's warm and smells so good. I don't get too near the boiling licorice."

"Same with me. I never get to go in the special white room where the mozzarella is made."

Vanda stopped where another path bisected the one they were on. "Remember this spot if you ever want to find me. I live about five minutes in the direction of the sunrise. Just walk that way until you smell the water buffalo."

Pasquale ambled back up the path. "You two are talking too much. Just like girls always are. It's going to take forever to get into town. I have things to do. Cats to see."

Uffa piped up. "That's okay. I know where we are. I can find my way home now."

"I'm coming with you," said Vanda. "I never get into town and I don't have to be home for an hour or so."

They parted company with the lascivious tomcat and within ten minutes came to a busy road that passed the village.

"I never come down this way," said Vanda. "It's too chaotic. I'm a country farm cat."

"It's actually pretty peaceful at the licorice factory," said Uffa, who led the way into the road when there were no cars passing.

Just at that moment a red Ferrari thundered down the highway. Vanda lost sight of Uffa who had crossed first.

"*Uffa*! Are you okay?"

"*Accidenti!* I almost went to join my mother. If I hadn't rolled into the ditch, I'd have been roadkill."

Vanda scampered to her side. "Are you hurt?"

"No, just shaken. Where did they think they were going? Nothing happens here. Nobody is ever late for anything."

"I recognize that car. It's at Pussipu's house sometimes. That was Don Pino. Pussipu calls him the 'Bad Man.' I wonder where he's going? I hope my friend is not going to have another chaotic night."

"Come on. Let's get away from here." Uffa led the way down an alley behind a bakery and a shop from which the aroma of fish and a deep fat fryer wafted.

They crossed the main piazza where four old men sat at a table outside the only café, playing a lively card game of *Scopa*. A toddler escaped his grandmother and tossed his small ball at the two cats. Uffa gave chase.

"Uffa, come on," called Vanda. "I don't know the way." She rubbed up against a bench, leaving a bit of scent. She wanted to find her way back home, so had been marking the route – lamp posts, doorways, and benches – as she went.

The young calico cat swerved back to the far corner of the square. After two more blocks they came to a large parking lot in front of a huge metal-covered open area with high piles of twisted dried thin snakes of wood. The smell of licorice permeated the air.

"This is wonderful," said Vanda. "I've never seen anything like it."

"This is my home," said Uffa pushing out her chest. She scurried across the parking lot and seemed to dive into the woody mountain.

When Vanda got closer she could see a low tunnel through the tangled roots, like a secret passage to a hidden land. Into this sweet smelling dusty world she followed Uffa until they reached the center of the pile. The space opened up to a cave big enough for four or five cats. Uffa had pulled or pushed in an old t-shirt, stained black in places, a shoe box and a large torn piece of foam rubber. Vanda thought of her comfortable window seat in the kitchen at home. She thought of Pussipu's tasseled cushion. She was amazed to see that Uffa was so cheerful.

"This place is so far back in the pile that they will never get to it when they haul roots into the chipping, shredding and crushing room. I think my little apartment is safe."

"But where is your bowl of kibble?"

"What's kibble?"

"Delicious dry food in many flavors – fish, beef, or chicken."

"Sounds boring. I like the richness of a fat mouse or the tang of a lizard."

"Yes, but…"

"I never eat back here anyway. I don't want ants or other bugs to come here and especially not any uninvited cats. I carry my meals to the end of the root pile, near the door. The foreman seems to like to see evidence of the mice and rats I catch. Like I'm earning my keep. Since they leave fresh water for me, I don't have to drink out of the fountain in the village piazza, like some cats do. You know dogs drink there, too. *Ewww.*"

"I understand, but…"

"I use this place only for naps and after I finish hunting at night. You never know what will pop out in the dark. I like to have the cover."

Vanda decided to stop criticizing the décor. "It seems kind of lonely. I can always find a lap to sit on at home."

"I'm not here that much. I'm out and about during the day and all of the workers have a nice word for me, except for the lady who works on the computer in the office. She smells like a dog. I don't think she likes our kind. Or maybe she's a bit afraid of me."

Vanda held up her white paw in disagreement. "That's too kind of you. Dog people are hopeless. Believe me, I know. Signora Esmeralda who is bad tempered, hates me and smells of cocker spaniel. I like to walk on her car when that dirty dog is inside. He always has a spasm."

"I'd love to see that."

"Come over any Tuesday morning," Vanda snickered. "You can help me."

They sat for a moment in silence, contemplating the torment of dogs, and then because they had nothing to say. Vanda scanned the small hovel again. Well, maybe she should…

"Let's get out of here," urged Uffa. "Do you want to see the cauldrons?"

"Do you get to go inside? I thought you said they discourage that."

Uffa led the way out of her home. "I know a secret way in. The workers are probably gone until tomorrow. We'll check. The shredded roots in the cauldrons are stirred and simmer for days before the licorice is done. I especially like to go in during the wintertime. It's nice and warm in there."

"I'd love to see it. I can't imagine how they get the roots to melt."

"It's all about cooking them forever."

"Forever?"

"Well, for days and days, at least." She waited for Vanda to emerge from the tunnel. "Let's check the cauldron room for humans."

Uffa led the way around the edge of the building to the back side where a pile of bricks against the wall provided access to a long narrow window running horizontally high on the wall.

Uffa leapt to the ledge and Vanda followed. Through the window they could see three huge cauldrons. The nearest was sending steam to the ceiling. A large metal paddle slowly mixed a thick mass of black.

"They are almost done with that batch," said Uffa. "See how thick it is."

A man entered the vast room from a door midway down one side of the room.

"That's Enrico. He's one of my favorites."

He climbed a ladder to a metal platform attached to the cauldron and reached inside with a long-handled hardwood spatula. He scooped out a blob of the black licorice and watched as it stretched in a long elastic band back into the mass.

"When it's cooked enough, they run it through a machine that flattens it into a long thin sheet. Then it goes through a cutter that chops it into pellets."

"That's much more interesting than watching mozzarella being made. It's all about hot water and blobs of cheese. Except I do like to watch them braid the *treccia* when the mozzarella is all stretchy."

"Maybe I can come over tomorrow and see that." Uffa jumped down to the ground, landing on all four feet. "Enrico's going home. Let's go inside."

Vanda trailed behind until they reached a hole in the wall.

"They haven't figured out that I use this little tunnel to get in and out of the factory. When they catch sight of me inside they always think I got in through an open door."

The metal pipe was a tight squeeze for Vanda.

Uffa explained, "It's for draining off the water when they hose out the room once a week. Then it's kind of dangerous because the water come gushing out into a ditch behind the building. I saw a family of mice swept away last year. I'm not sure if they were inside or out when the flood came."

The room looked even bigger to Vanda when they were inside. The floor was polished cement. The walls were plastered and painted beige. The cauldrons were unpainted steel.

"Let's look at the middle one. The one we saw from the window is much too hot." Uffa bounded across the room. Vanda followed in a low-to-the-ground-trying-to-hide mode.

"I heard Enrico call the platform at the top a 'catwalk,'" said Uffa. "So it must be a good place for us."

Vanda thought that there wasn't much difference between the two cooking pots as they climbed the metal stairs to the narrow platform at the top of the central cauldron. It wasn't steaming as much as the one below the window, but the air rippled from the heat coming out of the liquid black mass being continually stirred by big metal paddles.

Vanda had just looked over the edge at the dark black hell cooking in the gigantic pot when Uffa's back foot slipped over the edge and her hip followed.

"*Aiiii*," the young cat caterwauled.

Vanda, who had never carried a kitten in her life, instinctively clamped her mouth onto the ruff of the back of Uffa's neck, pinching the loose skin while backing up. Uffa was a lot heavier than any kitten and gravity pulled her into the cauldron. Vanda extended her claws through the metal grate, trying for traction.

Uffa's back legs scrambled against the hot steel wall. She felt an intense burning at the tip of her tail and as the paddle came around, she made one last effort to push off the top of it onto the catwalk. She streaked down the stairs.

Vanda took one last look at the molten black goo and scurried after her. She found Uffa in a huge porcelain sink near their entry tunnel, sitting in three inches of water in which Enrico's wood paddle was soaking. The tip of Uffa's tail was coated in black licorice.

"What are you going to do with that?" Vanda sat on the soap dish, peering down at Uffa's sopping tail.

"Don't know," moaned Uffa. "Maybe it will get hard and just crack off, but probably it hadn't cooked enough so it will stay sticky and become a filthy ball. I think I'll lick on it for awhile."

"Wish I could help," Vanda smiled, relieved that her new friend was not seriously hurt. "But I have to go home before it gets too dark."

"I'd walk you to the main square, but I think I should deal with this."

"No need. I marked my way."

"But you don't know the town cats. They won't bother me, but they might take exception to you."

"I plan to be moving fast. They won't even know I was there."

The next morning Uffa came down the drive of the Caseificio Torre Mordillo just as Berto was herding the water buffalo into the yard from the milking barn. Uffa jumped onto the fence to get out of the way of the hoofs. If she put out a paw she could have touched the point of old Peppina's curved gray horn.

"Your timing couldn't be better," piped Vanda from the other side of the fence. "I'm about to get my morning milk in the shop. I'll share."

"I haven't had milk since my mother was killed. Even before her death she had been cutting back on the supply, if you know what I mean."

"You aren't lactose intolerant are you? Some cats get that way, you know?"

"Don't think so."

Marco came through the shop from the *cucina* where the mozzarella was made. He opened the door to find the two cats sitting patiently on the doorstep.

"Wait a minute Vanda. It's okay that you have a friend visit, but Pussipu is the one I know. She's had her shots and doesn't have fleas. This one may not be so fastidious," he said, blocking the doorway. He stared at the young calico. "She's cute, but there's something a bit strange about her tail." He looked like he was about to touch Uffa and then changed his mind. "So I'm going to serve the two of you out here on the steps."

Vanda glanced at Uffa's tail. Sure enough a glob of dusty licorice clung like a knob on the tip.

He went back in and came back with two bowls of fresh water buffalo-warm milk. He set them on either side of the stoop before going back in and shutting the door.

"Don't let it hurt your feelings. When he gets to know you, he'll be friendlier."

"That's all right. I'm used to eating *al fresco*." Uffa forced herself to lap the creamy milk slowly. It was so good. She wanted it to last as long as possible.

Vanda sat back when she was about half done. "Here take the rest of this. I'll get more this evening."

"I might be back up here for breakfast, tomorrow."

"Next time I'll finish my bowl, but you take it now."

Once they were sated, Vanda led them around the side of the building "Marco should be starting to make the *palle* and *treccie* now."

They jumped up on the window sill of the *cucina* windows.

"There's no way to get in there, so I can't give you a secret tour."

"Knowing me, it's probably safer."

"How does your tail feel?"

"It's getting better. At least the licorice hardened, so it's as clean as the rest of me. It'll crack off some day."

Vanda hid a smile. "You hope."

Through the windows they could see a white-tiled room. A round stainless steel vat of water was heating on one side of the room. On a gleaming metal table were loaves of porous cheese curd made from milk from the water buffalos during their morning milking the day before. Marco carved off a large piece of the curd, placed it in a large round metal pan and crumbled it into small pieces. He added scoops of hot water and stirred the melting crumbs with a wooden stick into a smooth mass.

"What he's doing is called 'stringing the curd.' Once, Angelica did it for a friend of hers in the kitchen of the house and I got to sit beside them and watch." Vanda explained. "All you need is hot water and some of the cheese from the loaf."

After the desired elasticity was achieved, Marco scooped off the excess water. From the large mass of mozzarella, he used the plastic scoop and the wooden stick to cut off baseball-sized pieces and dumped them into a rectangular bath of warm water where he formed them into balls of *mozzarella di bufala*.

"Those are called *palle di mozzarella di bufala*. Each loaf of cheese makes about twenty balls. They go into a salted bath to cool for a few hours. But they can be sold and eaten while they are still warm."

Marco then carved off a huge hunk of the smooth elastic mass. He warmed it by dipping it into the hot water bath. Then he held it high and let it stretch.

"He's making a *treccia*. That's my favorite one to watch him make."

He dipped the long piece into the warm water again and then let it stretch even more. Folding it over at the center, Marco began to twine the *treccia* into its classic braided form.

"He usually makes ten or so braids a day, some large and some small."

"Have you ever eaten the cheese?"

"Yes, but I like the fresh milk better. The mozzarella make me constipated."

"*Ewww.* Too much information, Vanda."

"Pretty sensitive for one who lives in a pile of roots, youngster." Vanda batted at Uffa's head causing her to fall off the window sill. She followed her down, landing with more grace.

"Let's go visit Pussipu's villa for our morning nap," Vanda suggested.

Uffa sucked a little on the licorice clump on her tail. She glanced sideways at Vanda. "Do you think we will find Pasquale on the way?"

"Forget that tomcat," Vanda retorted. "He will only get you into trouble."

"What do you mean?"

"You are just too young for a romantic life. Give yourself time to enjoy being a kid."

Uffa thought about this as she gave her tail a last lap. The button of licorice was now shiny black. "But he's just like a big kid."

"That's what I mean. No sense of responsibility." Vanda nudged her to her feet. "Come on. Let's go."

They wound up through the chaparral, enjoying the warm sunshine and light breeze. Uffa caught a lizard and carried it for awhile before letting it run off. A small shadow swept passed them and then back.

"*Duck*! Under the juniper bush!" Vanda pushed Uffa head over heels into the large tangled branches of the dark green shrub. An unearthly scream escalated and then dwindled.

"You are afraid of a duck?"

"No, it was a *falco*. You probably don't see those in town, but let me tell you it wasn't after me. I'm too fat. That raptor wanted you for lunch."

"Is it gone?"

"Probably, but let's keep in the trees and move fast. We can rest when we get to the villa."

Vanda led the way, racing up the hill, weaving in and out of the olive trees and rosemary bushes. They were out of breath when they got up to the villa, at the end of a narrow dirt road, behind a wrought iron fence. They slipped through the bars and padded through a sculpted garden with low hedges of lavender plants and terracotta pots with miniature lemon and orange trees. After they rounded the house she looked up to see if Pussipu was in her window.

She was. Upon seeing the two breathless cats she patted the window with her paw and disappeared.

"She'll meet us by the laundry room door," Vanda said as she led the way to an open door, covered by a curtain, on the lower level of the house.

"I'm so glad you two came to visit," said Pussipu, slipping her head under the curtain. "Come in. Tommaso is still sleeping. He goes back to the university in two days. I'm going to miss him."

"Is his mother home?"

"Signora Amelia is out at the market. The housekeeper is taking a day off. Come in. Come in." She ducked back under the curtain.

"Wow! This is the first human home I've ever been in," said Uffa, gazing around at the blue and white tiled laundry room.

"Wait until you see upstairs," laughed Vanda as they scampered up the steps following Pussipu.

They came out in the kitchen. The brown Persian nosed over an aromatic plate on a plastic mat on the floor beside the refrigerator

"I've left some sardines if you want a snack. Signora is going to make shrimp scampi tonight, so I want to save room."

Uffa's green eyes gleamed. She gobbled the fish, but Vanda was more thirsty after the run up the hill. She went to Pussipu's water bowl.

Uffa explored the kitchen while munching on a sardine tail. "This whole room is just for food? It looks as big as a house to me."

"You'll have to tour the other rooms," said Vanda after she finished drinking. She turned to Pussipu. "Why is Tommaso sleeping? The sun has been up for hours."

"There was another horrible fight here last night. Don Pino…"

Vanda interrupted, "He almost ran us down on the road by the village."

"When?"

"Last evening. He was driving that fancy red car of his like a hawk after a rabbit. Uffa and I were almost roadkill."

The brown Persian nodded. "He must have been coming back here. He argued with Tommaso for hours, saying that he had to leave medical school in Rome and come back here to work for the family." She continued talking as she led the way down the hall. "I would love to have Tommaso stay here all of the time, but I could see that the idea was making him very unhappy. He kept saying that times changed and traditions die, whatever that means. Then he said he had to follow his heart. I know what that means."

She nudged open a partially cracked door. "Uffa, this is my powder room. If you ever need a little sand and don't want to go outside, come here."

"Jeepers," said Uffa. "They give you a room just for that?" She looked around the tiled room with white porcelain fixtures and stuck her nose in a blue plastic dome- covered box of kitty litter.

"I have to share the room with guests when the Signora or Tommaso have friends come over. You can still smell Don Pino's horrible scent. I only wish there was a window."

"So how did the fight end, Pussipu?" Vanda stayed in the hall.

"Don Pino threatened to put Tommaso in the hospital, but not as a doctor. He tried to punch Tommaso, but Signora Amelia came in holding the gun they use to shoot feral dogs. She told Don Pino to leave and never come back. She said he had already taken too much from her. That she wasn't going to lose Tommaso, too."

"Wow," Uffa said. "You should have jumped on his head and bitten his ear."

"I wish I had. I expect that was the last chance I'll have to draw blood from that awful excuse for a human being." She led the way into a big cool room, painted in peach tones, with a bed topped with a cut-lace spread and a honey-colored cashmere throw folded at the foot. "I get to sleep up there as long as I don't spread my claws on the lace. The Signora likes to have me purr while she is falling asleep. After she is in dreamland, I wander the house. I'm more of a napper. Speaking of which would you like to join me for a pre-lunch snooze."

Vanda nodded. "After our run-in with the hawk, I think…"

"What hawk?"

Uffa laughed. "We didn't tell you. Vanda thought I was almost breakfast for a hawk this morning. I didn't see a thing, but we ran almost all the way up the valley, so it didn't get a second chance at me."

"I hate hawks. The vultures are almost as bad, but they seem to like their meals dead instead of with a beating heart, plucked out of a torn chest."

"Ugg, Pussipu. I don't think I'll be able to get that out of my mind."

They retraced their path down the hall and into the vast living room. Uffa stopped open-mouthed.

"It never ends. This is like the best dream I ever had, but I never knew this world existed. Imagine you live here all by yourself. An only cat."

"I'm lonely sometimes. But mostly at night. Tommaso is gone a lot. It might be nice to have a friend."

"You have Vanda and now, you have me."

Pussipu jumped up on her window pillow. "Come up here. There's plenty of room. The view is marvelous." She winked at Vanda. "I think I can see your hawk circling."

"So long as there is glass between that raptor and me, I can sleep."

"What about the 'bird' down there in that tree?" Uffa said, her eyes gleaming.

Passipu looked down at the olive trees lining the driveway. "Pasquale! Did he follow you?" The big orange and black tabby gazed up at them from a comfortable fork in the branches.

"Not that we know of," said Vanda. "It's good we have glass between him and us, too."

The three friends curled around each other into a mound of cats and fell asleep.

It could have been minute or it could have been hours when a yowl of a cat and the scream of a man woke Vanda. It could have been a nightmare or real, she didn't know. She opened her eyes to gaze out at the view. But the view was gone. *The clouds have moved in to cover the hilltop*, she thought. *Time to be heading home.*

She heard a sound of the kitchen door opening. *Signora Amelia must be back*, she mused. *I wonder what's for lunch.*

The figure who walked into down the hall wasn't Tommaso's plump mother. It was a tall skinny man. Blood dripped down his head from scratches over his left ear. He was carrying a knife and a gas can.

Vanda kicked out at Pussipu. "Do you know him?" she hissed in one tufted ear.

"It's Don Pino's son Alberto," Pussipu said in disdain. "Why is he here? Why is he bleeding?"

"I think Pasquale did that," Vanda said, remembering her dream.

"What's cooking?" asked Uffa, stretching. "I smell smoke."

Vanda stared out the window. Not clouds. Smoke.

Pasquale burst out of the kitchen into the *sala*. "You've got to get out of here. I tried to stop him. Didn't you hear me? The house is on fire!" he cried at the same time that Pussipu caterwauled, "*Tommaso*! I have to save Tommaso!"

The Persian streaked after Alberto and reached his bare ankles, shod in Gucci loafers, just as he got to Tommaso's bedroom door. She speared his left foot with all of her front claws and then clamped on tight with a whole mouthful of teeth. He screamed as he pushed through the door, dropping the open gas can so that the fuel spilled down the hallway.

Tommaso leaped out of bed, dressed only in a t-shirt and briefs. He ducked the slashing knife and punched his cousin in the stomach. Alberto dropped the knife, landing on his back in the hall. Pussipu, claws extended, leaped on his face. He screamed again.

"Pussipu," Pasquale called. "The *fire*! We have to get out of here."

At the same time Tommaso noticed the smoke billowing up the big front picture window. "You idiot," he said. "You set the fire first and then come to kill me. No wonder your father wanted me to stay and take over the family business." He pulled Alberto up by his jacket, set him on his feet and pushed him down the hall to the kitchen. "Pussipu, get outside." He almost tripped as four cats pushed past his feet and out the kitchen door.

Outside they could see that the entire front of the house was in flames. There was an explosion from the lower level.

Tommaso demanded that Alberto hand over his jacket and his phone. Tommaso called the fire department and reported the blaze. Alberto ran for his car and took off down the road. "Idiot! Does he think he's going to get away?" Tommaso said to the four cats sitting at his feet. They, of course, assuming the question was rhetorical, didn't respond.

A whoosh of sound from inside the house told them that the fire had climbed the laundry room steps and found the gasoline in the hall. As the cats followed Tommaso down to the entry gate, they could hear the siren of a fire truck making its way up the valley.

Pussipu turned to her two friends. "Vanda, you and Uffa should go to the dairy. I may come by later."

"I'm staying with you, *Principessa*," Pasquale said. "You shouldn't be alone. Alberto may come back."

"Of course you can stay, my hero." Pussipu licked the soot off his brow.

Pasquale may have found the way to her heart, Vanda thought as she followed Uffa down the path. *At least for tonight.*

Nine weeks later, Vanda made her way to the licorice factory. Crawling through the tunnel of fragrant twisted roots, she heard peeps and squeaks, like a family of mice had moved in with Uffa. As she came into the cave she found Uffa and her brood of four sightless kits. Three girls and a boy.

"That one looks just like his father," Vanda said, nosing the tabby kitten. "I told you that you weren't ready for love."

"Well, I'm definitely not ready for this brood."

"Now cheer up," Vanda said with a chuckle. "At least they're cute. And you won't be lonely."

"Look at my figure," Uffa moaned. "I'm all stretched out. Even the workers have noticed."

"I'm sure they saw the pregnant belly before they noticed that you lack your usual toned tummy."

"No they didn't. I never went out in the daytime for the last four weeks. Now I have to because I can't leave this bunch for hours at a time." Uffa rearranged herself into a more comfortable position and her brood crawled in to feed. "Enough complaining. I'm sure I will come to love them all. Tell me what happened to Pussipu."

"Of course you will love them. What's not to love? Especially after their eyes open." Vanda folded her legs under her chest. "Pussipu stayed with us for a couple of days. Then Tommaso came and got her. He and his mother are moving to Rome for good. Pussipu is going to have to acquire a Roman accent and learn big city ways."

"I guess we won't see her again."

"Maybe not. Tommaso and Signora Amelia still own the villa but it is a burnt out hull. Pussipu heard that they plan to sell the land to an American who wants to build a small hotel and spa, whatever that is."

"I've heard about America. They show movies from there outside in the piazza in the summertime. I wonder if my babies might find a rich tourist who will take them home to Hollywood or New York."

"Why not? With a mother like you and an aunt like me, they will be able be anything they want to be and go where they want to go."

The ship's horn blew as they left port.

Vanda had been misled. Pussipu wasn't going to acquire a Roman accent. She was going to learn an entirely new cat language, an American one. The chocolate brown Persian hadn't meant to lie, but she learned of the new destination herself only when Tommaso carried her up the gang plank in the Civitavecchia cruise port.

Little did she know that this would be the easiest part of the trip. Once they got to Barcelona they would catch a plane to New York where Tommaso would continue his studies at Cornell Medical College.

"Pussipu, *ecco la tua cena*," said Signora Amelia, sliding a small platter of liver pâté topped with anchovies onto the balcony where Pussipu sat in a round upholstered wicker chair practicing mindfulness, breathing in and out and in again.

Would the next tale of the *Cats of Italy* be *Italian Cats in America?*

THE AUTHOR

For sixteen years, Ann Reavis avoided practicing law in San Francisco by living in Florence, Italy with Dante and Guido, two feline friends. There she worked as a tour guide and maintained a website – TuscanTaveler.com – about Italian culture and food (two of her passions).

Now she lives in Washington, DC and writes about her Italian experiences in *Italian Food Rules* and *Italian Life Rules* and in novels and short stories – *Death at the Duomo* and *Cats of Italy*.

Made in the USA
San Bernardino, CA
06 March 2017